THESE GREAT ATHENIANS

Retold Passages for Seldom Heard Voices

THESE GREAT ATHENIANS

Retold Passages for Seldom Heard Voices

Valentine Carter

TWENTY SEVEN

First edition published in 2021 by Imprint Twenty Seven,

an imprint of Nobrow Ltd. 27 Westgate Street, London, E8 3RL.

Design by Emily Sear

Printed and bound by Ozgraf, Poland on FSC® certified paper.

ISBN: 9781914343001

www.imprint27.com

www.nobrow.net

'For there are no new ideas. There are only new ways of making them felt – of examining what those ideas feel like being lived [...] while we suffer the old longings, battle the old warnings and fears of being silent and impotent and alone, while we taste new possibilities and strengths.'

Audre Lorde

... tell the old story for our modern times.

Find the beginning.

Homer's *Odyssey*

PREFACE

Homer's *Odyssey* contains moments of extreme violence, of horror in all its forms. Some of it still seems quite inventive to me. I remember this coming as a shock to my much younger self on reading the full version, as my first introduction to the myth had been the benevolent extract in *The Faber Book of Greek Legends*. It was adapted for children and it was wonderful. But it did not prepare me for the original.

I hesitate to describe any version of *The Odyssey* as original. There is the issue of form; these myths were part of the oral tradition and then recorded in writing later. Also, of provenance. When manuscripts were shipped to the Great Library of Alexandria for preservation, the librarians there rewrote some sections so they would be considered more appropriate in Alexandrian society. If we are reading the myth in the English language, we also have to consider these versions as translations, moving us yet further from the notional original. But this is part of the joy of mythology. Myths are told by many voices, in many ways and those voices sound different depending on where – and when – they are from. As Marina Warner points out, 'Every telling of a myth is part of that myth: there is no Ur-version, no authentic prototype, no true account.' Because I was the kind of kid who was left to their own devices, and because I spent a lot of time with my head either in a book or in the clouds, I made up my own versions of the Greek myths. I fixed things I didn't like, I stood in for characters and did things the way I thought they should be done. I am not too proud to tell you that I galloped above the fields on Pegasus, only returning him to the stars when I had to come in for tea. Which was fine, because everyone has very regular mealtimes in the myths too. It's part of the form.

I think, in the technicolour of hindsight, one of the things I enjoyed most about my story book of Greek myths was that all the people in them were, like me, at odds with the world in which they found themselves. How, they wondered, had they landed there, and what were they supposed to do now they had? Where I had come from, where I was and where I was going were all questions that concerned me. And now I'm still asking: What is my past? What is my present? And what do the past and the present tell me about my future? An answer to all those questions might mean you have the answer to another question: Who am I? This is the principal business of myth.

These questions open up spaces, and there is a home in these myths for people who aren't living comfortably in our hyper heteronormative world. There are women who live important moments as men, humans who turn into animals, gods who can transport themselves halfway around the world in the blink of an eye. Everything is different and everything is possible. But as I grew up, navigating the choppy waters of adolescence, and as I graduated on to the adult texts from the Big Library in Town, I realised that this home in myth is, as in the real world, hard fought for. It is a way of seeing, not the way things are. The existence of this difference is not something everyone is made to understand.

Marcel Detienne described myths as 'good to think with'. We can use them as a lens to take another, perhaps differently angled, look at the things around us right now. One way of doing this is by thinking radically about the stories and the characters that populate them.

I think it's important that we do this, rather than just regurgitate the 'original' text. Partly because, as I came to understand, there *isn't* an original text, not even the canonical one which has been assessed and lauded by straight white men of wealth. But more importantly, because myths are concerned with what the past and the present can tell us about the future. Perhaps we should consider whether we have reached a point where the old ways of telling these stories no longer reflect our present. Should we continue to allow these stories to peddle nonsense like *sex sways all women's minds* (Book 15: 421), or *slaves are lucky* (Book 15: 448), unchallenged or unopposed? I think we need to take responsibility for these ideas, now more than ever.

The stories that most interest me in *The Odyssey* are the women's stories. This is partly because they are so mysterious, so often unfinished.

There is Penelope, who doesn't know if her husband is alive or dead, only that he's been gone for two decades. She rules without Odysseus until her son is old enough to take over, holding at bay a house full of men who are demanding she marry one of them. She promises that she will, but only once she has woven a shroud for her father-in-law. She spends all her days weaving it and then, cleverly, unpicks it every night so that it will never be finished. There is Circe, who turns the men who invade her island into pigs. Calypso, who knows how to get back to Ithaca, how to make boats, even how to appease the gods. They both weave. Athena, who can do anything, go anywhere, who invented weaving. Melantho, who just keeps going when it seems impossible to do so. Scylla, my favourite. Scylla eats men. Dawn who threads the days together. And all the women in Hades who have died, who have, like Dawn, held life steady. But one thing that is striking to me about these women is that none of them speak to each other in *The Odyssey*. They are isolated. They are also enslaved, exiled, cursed, blamed, threatened, brutalised, terrorised, raped and murdered. They never communicate with each other, not about these abuses or anything else. They are friendless. And in that, they are ultimately powerless. Odysseus' power and agency comes from his companions. (Well, mostly it comes from Athena – but he doesn't do anything on his own. Apart from nearly drowning a few times.) But if these women were friends, if they did meet, what would they talk about? What would they have to say for themselves? Do we know them well enough? Do they know themselves well enough to reach out to someone else and know them too? I don't think so.

Let's imagine what Calypso might really think of Odysseus. Let's think about Melantho and what her day looks like with a house full of violent, out of control men.

And so I have taken my cue from the weavers, these women with their strong, capable hands. I have unravelled Homer's work and remade it into something that begins to answer that original question: Who am I? Perhaps if enough individuals try to find the answer to that question we will begin to find a space where we can answer another, perhaps better question: Who are we?

It will take courage to embark on these kinds of journeys, but I find it comforting to think that if there is no authentic original, if every telling becomes part of the myth, then no one should have authority over the tellings – everyone has a right to their own version.

In that spirit, this version is mine. From it you can weave your own, if you have a need to.

Voices

(in alphabetical order)

Alcmene
Anticleia
Ariadne
Athena
Calypso
Circe
Dawn
Epicaste
Eriphyle
Maera
Megara
Melantho
Penelope
Phaedra
Scylla
Tyro

PENELOPE

ITHACA

YARN

Penelope waits. And she weaves. She weaves
because there is a meditation in this
back and forth, this captured time like a held breath
in the night. Her hands, occupied with this flying
shuttle, are sure and deft yet her eyes seek the
unseeing middle distances. Stillness.
The burial shroud, wrapping for an abandoned
father, grows beneath the weft and warp. At this
loom she waits for a death and for a return.
Or for two deaths. One done and one incomplete,
a body fallen to Ares, a body lost
to Poseidon perhaps. Odysseus.
Is he now her coin-eyed boy? Who can
know? Waiting is indecision measured in
anxious paces across a marble floor.

Yet it is hope that treadles this loom, weaves
this cloth, shrouds this life in pauses, in this thought:
Come back home, come back home or we will come
to hate you.

Penelope is surrounded, alone.
Her house is riotous with uncalled-for suitors.
Unknown shadows leap along walls, shudder
beneath candle flames that long to burn in vigil
forever. This house is no longer a home, more
Charon's ferry stalled mid-Acheron, sweet
tributary of death. And so back to that, then,
to death again. To the inevitable. Perhaps.

She is safe for now, in this room, their room
with their bed threaded into the olive tree,
the tree with roots woven into the foundations
of this house. Their room is as inviolable
as the tides that refuse to send him back.
She is only safe while the weaving remains
in this state of being done.

While it is
unfinished she is still wife, mother, lover,
bereft, left, Penelope, beloved, fidelity,
she, woman, her, woman. Collapsing inwards
under the weight of expectant convention.

She is snagged, a tangled thread caught in the
beater, knotted in the ratchet as the cloth
fills the winding roller unperturbed. No
matter. She will unpick her handiwork before morning.

And come that morning all this, all of the
anticipation and indecision will fall
upon her, snarling, until nothing remains
except the stilled, empty beams of this silent
loom.

Loss is always unfinished anyway

WEFT

Penelope waits. And she seethes. She seethes
because there is no escape from this back and
forth, this restless time like an unwanted other,
breathing heavily in the night. Her hands, occupied
with the flying shuttle, are as thoughtless and
automatic as her eyes that shun the soft
grey of sleep. Relentless. The burial shroud,
wrapping for an abandoned life, grows beneath
the weft and warp. At this loom she must wait
for a death and for a return. Or for two deaths. One
done and one incomplete, a body fallen to
Ares, a body lost to Poseidon perhaps.
Odysseus. Is he now her coin-eyed boy?
Who can know? Waiting is postponement,
left to stretch like evening shadows across the
parched meadow of Asphodel.

                                Yet it is
anger that treadles this loom, weaves this cloth,
shrouds this life in pause, in this thought. *Leave me then.*
Leave me to them and be done with it.

Penelope is besieged, abandoned. Her
son's house is riotous with uncalled-for suitors.
Unknown boots cross thresholds, block doorways closing
against them. Her refusals ring unheard until
their hollow echoes die in dark corners, in
stairwells. This house is no longer a home, more
Charon's ferry stranded in the Styx, that sweet
tributary of death. And so back to that
then, to death again. To the inevitable. Perhaps.

She is not safe, in this room, their room
where their bed threaded into the tree, the tree
with roots woven into the foundations
of their home, winds its constricting memories
around her body. Their room is as inviolable
as the tides that refuse to send Odysseus
back. She is not safe while this funereal
weaving inches towards a state of being done.

While it is unfinished, she is still wife,
mother, lover, bereft, left, Penelope,
bereft, she, woman, left, her, woman. Collapsing
inwards under the weight of expectant
convention. Woman. Not-woman.

She is trapped there, a tangled thread caught in the
beater, knotted in the ratchet as the cloth
chokes the winding roller, unrelenting. No
matter. She will unravel herself before morning.

And come that morning all this, all of the
hurt and injustice will fall upon her, howling,
until nothing remains except the stilled and
empty beams of this silent loom.

                              Loss is
always unfinished anyway

Penelope dreams. And she sees. She sees
the miles and miles of ocean, empty tides
rolling back and forth, restless, wine-dark seas
as unforgiving as night. Her sleeping hands,
occupied with this twisted sheet, are as
thoughtless and automatic as her eyes that
search for the soft arms of sleep. Restless. The
burial shroud, wrapping for an abandoned
life, lies undone beneath the weft and warp. In
this bed she must wait for a death and for a
return. Or for two deaths. One done and one
incomplete, a body shredded on a
battlefield, a body bloated on an ocean
floor. Odysseus. Is he now some coin-eyed
monster? Who will care? Waiting is dread
suspended, Penelope is left to
swing beneath the gallows of lives unfinished.

In sleep fear still treadles this loom, still weaves
this cloth, shrouds this life in pause, in this thought:
*If I could wake, if I could wake, come morning this
would end.*

Penelope is asleep, abandoned.
This dark house is riotous with uncalled-for
monsters. Unknown footsteps sound in hallways,
breezes stir where no wind reaches. These ghosts cry
unheard until their hollow echoes die in
dark corners, in stairwells. This house is no
longer a home, more Charon's ferry stranded
in the Styx, sweet tributary of death. And

so back to that then, to death again. To the
stalking dread.

                  She is not safe, in this sleep, this
sleep in their bed that was threaded into the
tree, the tree with roots woven into the
foundations of their home but now cut loose,
casting her into ill-lit memories as yet unmade.
Their room was inviolable as the tides
that refuse to send Odysseus back. She
is dreaming of distances unfathomable
and outcomes unthinkable.

                      But while she dreams
she is still wife, mother, lover, bereft, left,
Penelope, bereft, she, woman, left, her,
woman. Collapsing inwards under the weight
of expectant convention. Woman. Not-woman.

She is trapped there, a battered skiff caught
in the undertow, smashed against the waves as
the sea engulfs the listing vessel
unrelenting. No matter. She will unravel
herself before morning.

                   And come that morning
all this, all the terror and foreboding will
fall upon her, clawing, until nothing remains
except the stilled and empty sails of this abandoned
ship.

        Loss is always unfinished anyway

FASTNESS

Penelope waits. And she unravels.
She unravels fathoms of cloth, busy
fingers twitching here and there, restless in
the night hours that lean into the pale light
of dawn. Her hands, occupied now with the
unravelling, are as calculating and
determined as the eyes that shun the grey
of sleep. Fearful. The burial shroud, wrapping
for an abandoned life, lies undone beneath
the weft and warp. We must wait for a death and
for a return. Or for two deaths. One done and
one incomplete. An Odysseus always
unfinished. Destined to be revisited,
repeated. Always searched for yet always
unfound. Is he now my coin-eyed boy?
Have I stolen him? I do not want him.
Penelope waits while my patience speeds
away like a schooner through violet waves.

Yet it is deviousness that treadles this
loom, still weaves this cloth, shrouds this life in pause,
in this thought: *If I were you, what would I do?*
Would I hold on to myself while the centre spins
off course?

Penelope is pitied, abandoned.
This dark house is riotous with uncalled-for
monsters. Unknown footsteps sound in hallways,
breezes stir where no wind reaches. Her ghost cries
unheard until the hollow echoes die in
dark corners, in stairwells. This woman is no
longer a woman, more fidelity's muse
stranded in this saccharine tribute to death.

And so back to that then, to death again. To
the inevitable. Perhaps.

                    She is not
whole, in this story, his story begun in
their bed that is threaded into the tree,
the tree with roots woven into the foundations
of their home but now cut loose, casting her
into splintered memories as yet unmade.
Her room is as unknowable as the Fates
that refuse to send Odysseus back.
I am dreaming of distances incalculable
and outcomes unthinkable.

                    But while I dream
she is still wife, mother, lover, bereft, left,
Penelope, bereft, she, woman, left, her,
woman. Collapsing inwards under the weight
of expectant convention. Not-woman. And what am I?

She is trapped here, a battered skiff caught in
the undertow, smashed against the waves as
the sea engulfs the listing vessel
unrelenting. No matter. I can unravel
her before morning.

                    And come that morning all
this, all the speculation and assumption
will fall upon her, gnawing, until nothing
remains except the stilled, empty sails of an
abandoned ship.

                    Loss is always unfinished
anyway

Penelope wonders. And she unravels.
She unravels fathoms of cloth, busy
fingers twitching here and there, restless in
the night hours that lean into the pale light
of dawn. Her hands, occupied now with the
unravelling, are as calculating and
determined as the eyes that shun the black depths
of sleep. Fearless. The burial shroud, wrapping
for an abandoned life, lies undone beneath
the weft and warp. Amongst this thread must we wait
for a death and for a return? Or for two
deaths. One done and one incomplete. An Odysseus
always unfinished. But gone, for all that.
Destined never to return. Seldom searched for
anymore. Have I stolen him? I do not
want him. Penelope wonders while her hope
carries her away like a schooner through
salted waves.

        Why is it necessary to
treadle this loom, still weave this cloth, shroud this life
in pause, when there is this thought: *If I were her,*
I would hold to myself, my centre spinning
off course, yes, but not beholden. Not like her.

But Penelope is freed in abandonment.
This dark house is riotous with unheeded
monsters. Her footsteps could sound in hallways, her
rightful places. Her words could be heard until
they echo through histories. This woman is
no longer a woman, more a mist rising

on a rare morning above the Styx. And so
back to that then, to death again. To the
inevitable.

No more. She could become
whole, in this story, her story begun in
their bed that is threaded into the tree, the
tree with roots woven into the foundations
of their home but now growing up and away
into indigo skies. Her fate is as unknowable
as that of Odysseus who may never
come back. We are dreaming of distances
incalculable and outcomes unthinkable.

And I dream too that she is no longer wife,
mother, lover, bereft, left, Penelope,
bereft, she, woman, left, her, woman. No longer
collapsing inwards under the weight of
expectant convention. Not-woman. Then what?
Now what?

She could be capable, a sharpened
blade pressed against the world that will deny her.
No doubt. She too could be changed by morning.

And come that morning all this, all the wonder
and possibility will fall upon her,
dancing, until nothing remains of this
coin-eyed boy except the distant toiling of
an abandoned ship.

Loss is always unfinished
anyway

TWIST

I wait. And Penelope weaves. Then she
unravels fathoms of cloth, busy fingers
twitching here and there, restless in the night hours
that lean into the pale light of dawn. My thoughts,
occupied now with her unravelling, are
as calculating and devious as her
hands, hands that work to save a life. Endless. The
burial shroud, wrapping for a rewound story,
lies undone beneath these hands. Among this thread
must I wait still for a death and for a return?
Or for two deaths. One done and one incomplete.
An Odysseus always unfinished.
But gone, for all that. Destined never to return.
Seldom searched for anymore. Have I murdered
him? I wait while Penelope's hope carries her
away like a schooner through salted waves.

Why is it necessary to treadle this tale,
still weave these words, shroud this life in theories,
when there is this thought: *Although I am not her,
I am like her, a centre spun off course.* Always
in flight, in motion. Stories are not told in
silence.

      Penelope is hidden, unknown.
This dark house is riotous with unfounded
speculations. I will make my footsteps sound
in hallways, my rightful places. My words will
be heard until they echo through these stories.
This woman is no longer a woman, more
a mist rising on a still morning, above the
ocean.

We will become whole, in this story,
her story begun in that bed threaded into
the tree, the tree with roots woven into the
foundations of this house but now growing up
and away into brightening skies. Her fate
is unknowable, not like that of Odysseus,
his fate rewritten. I am the one dreaming of
distances incalculable and outcomes
unthinkable.

And I promise this: she is
not only wife, mother, lover, bereft,
left, Penelope, bereft, she, woman, left,
her, woman. No longer collapsing inwards
under the weight of expectant convention.
Not-woman. Something else.

She is capable,
and now I am the sharpened blade pressed against
the world that would deny her. No doubt. I can
complete my handiwork before morning.

And come that morning all this, all these hesitant
words and this stuttering metre will fall
upon her, sinking, until nothing remains
of them but the insistent hope of an
abandoned woman.

Loss is always unfinished
anyway

SETT

Penelope weaves. And I unravel.
I unravel pages and pages of story,
busy fingers twitching here and there, restless
in the long hours that lean into the still
dark of night. My thoughts, occupied now with my
own unravelling, are as restless and tentative
as her thoughts, thoughts that work to save a life.
Doubtful. The burial shroud, wrapping for an
untold story, lies forgotten beneath some loom.
Among these threads must I still wait for a death
and for a return? Or for one death. Not one
done and one incomplete. My story always
unfinished. Always in the telling. Destined
to remain untold. Seldom searched for.
Will I abandon her? Will I watch while
Penelope's hope is worn to tattered threads?

Why is it necessary to treadle this tale,
still weave these words, shroud this life in theories?
A thought. *Perhaps I am like this too,*
my centre spinning off course while life slips
beneath the horizon. Stories are not told
in silence.

       I could stay hidden. My dark house
loud with unfounded speculations.
Unknown footsteps sound in hallways, breezes
stir where no wind reaches. Ghosts cry unheard
until the hollow echoes sound as songs.
This woman would no longer be a woman,
more a mist rising, still mourning above the ocean.

I will become whole, in this story
begun with that shroud threaded on a loom,
a shroud with threads reused over and over
now lying undone under brightening
skies. My fate is unknowable, not like that
of Odysseus who does come back. I am
the one dreaming of distances incalculable
and outcomes unthinkable.

                    And I promise
we will not be wife, mother, lover, bereft,
left, Penelope, bereft, she, woman, left,
her, woman. Never collapsing inwards under
the weight of expectant convention. We will
be an unexpected contradiction.

I am unstoppable, I am a sharpened
blade pressed against a world that would deny me.
No question. I can remake my handiwork
before morning.

                And come that morning all this,
all these hesitant words and this stuttering
metre will fly from me, soaring, until
nothing remains of them except the quiet taste
of salt on the breeze.

                  Loss is always unfinished
anyway

FIGURE

Penelope fades. And I gather. I gather
pages and pages of a story, busy
fingers twitching here and there, restless in the
long hours that lean into the still dark of night.
My thoughts, occupied now with this collecting,
are as calculating and determined as
her unpicking, unravelling to save
a life. Doubtless. This began with a burial
shroud, wrapping for an unnamed father, who now
lies forgotten alongside others. A shroud
and a death and a return. A return. At once
done and undone. A story is always
unfinished anyway. But done, for all that.
I will not abandon her. I will not
watch while Penelope's hope is worn
down to hang in tattered threads.

                    Why is it
necessary to treadle this tale, still weave
these words, shroud this life in theories? A thought:
Perhaps I am like this, my centre spun
off course while life promises escape over
the horizon. Stories are not told in silence.

I am hidden, unknown. My bright house is
riotous with unfounded speculations.
Unknown footsteps sound in hallways, breezes stir
where no wind reaches. Guests shout uninhibited
until the echoes sound as stories. These words
are no longer words, now no more than a
mist rising on a warm morning above the
ocean.

I could become whole in this story
but, honestly, I would rather remain
unfinished like a shroud now lying undone
under brightened skies. My fate unseen until
it emerges from shapes remembered. I am
still dreaming of distances incalculable
and outcomes unthinkable.

                    And I promise
we will never collapse inwards under
the weight of expectant convention. We will
be an unexpected contradiction.
We will be undeniable. A sharpened
blade pressed against the world. Always remade
before morning.

          And come that morning all this, these
still pages and writhing marks, will fly from me,
escaping, until nothing remains of them
except the quiet sting of salt on the skin.

& how gymnastic love's time is,
yesterday still warm against our skin
yet years ago, far beyond last week
or the cool, low-slung light of autumn
evenings spent walking in ambered woods

CALYPSO

AXE

Here you are, Calypso, gift-wrapped by firelight
& waiting for the night to fall as shadows
lengthen at the edges of your forests, darkening
the alders, the poplars & the cedar-scented cypress.
You wait at your loom for Odysseus to come back, drunk
on brine & sea-wind. His footsteps are heavy with grief,
he lags like a tired child burdened by too heavy a
woe. You hear him push aside the vines at your doorway
with a sigh that could whiten the crests of waves & wonder
is this all a hero is now, a man who finds
his way home? & what of you on your island throne?
This is more than a home; this is your kingdom.
Perhaps exile is the price you pay for wisdom
& this home-hungry man is not wise enough to stay.

ADZE

Here you are, Calypso, gift-wrapped by firelight
& waiting for night to fall as silence
slips across your broad forests, bringing such stillness
all the secretive creatures of darkness emerge.
You listen to Odysseus snuffle & huff
as if he would be better housed outside under
a root or fallen branch, moss-bound & damp
in the quiet air. You hear him push aside the food
& wine with a groan that rattles plates, cutlery.
Is this all a hero is now, a man who finds
fault in everything he touches? & what of you?
This is more than a home; this is your kingdom.
Perhaps loneliness is the price you'll pay for love
when this home-hungry man is not wise enough to stay.

GIMLET

Here you are, Calypso, shrink-wrapped by firelight
& waiting for a voice to sound, but silence
has crept into your home, stealing all your words
as secretively he sits brooding by your hearth.
You listen for some outside noise, an owl or fox
to break the deadening quiet that even
kindling won't disturb as the blazing flames leap
& dance. You hear him as an absence now, he is
becoming lost to you, like a tune from long ago.
Is this how things are now? A life shrouded in
dull lament & sour complaint. But what of you?
You are more than him, you are immortal. A Titan.
Perhaps boredom is the price you'll pay for love
when this too-human man runs out of charms.

POPLAR

Here you are, Calypso, trapped by this long night,
waiting for Dawn to come & start the day again
like a brand-new shuttle singing on your golden loom
as he weeps for the other weaver left behind.
You half-listen to his soft snoring, murmuring
in a dream as he laments an unkind current
that holds him just out of reach of home like a too-
short child before a high shelf. You had almost forgotten
that you saved him, plucked him from the cruellest current.
Is this how things are now? A debt dismissed,
as if these things are commonplace, as if *you* are.
You are more than he sees. You are immortal.
Perhaps disappointment is the price you'll pay
for hoping this too-human man would value honour.

ALDER

Where are you, Calypso, caught by this wondering,
these too-tight chains of thought that morning breaks
with the bright hope of dawn, rising to light your island
as the scent of cedar fills the forest air?
You watch Odysseus amble like a drunken
bear between the springs & the shore, or rather to
the full-fathomed sea beyond, to gaze blind with loss
homewards, his back towards you. You had almost forgotten
the sound of merry feet, of a fellow god, of Hermes.
& what does he want? For you to cede to another
man, a god, yes, but still male, still male. Not a woman.
You are more than they see, you are a Titan, Oceanid.
Perhaps disappointment is the price you'll pay
for hoping these not-human men would honour any woman.

FIR

Where are you, Calypso, caught by this wondering,
these too-tight chains of thought morning cannot
break, still bound by anger under the rising sun
as the scent of cedar fills the forest air?
You watch as Hermes skips into the sky, vanishing.
Mission done, missive told, mistress put in her place
like a drawer rammed into a chest,
far too full to shut. You had almost forgotten
the sound of men, of instructions, of ultimatums.
& what will you do now? What would I do now?
You are wedged into the world of men, a place to which
I will not follow you, for fear of getting stuck. If you are
misunderstood it's the price they make you pay
for hoping that they can change like skies at dawn.

CAULK

Who are you, Calypso, to be caught by this wondering?
These too-tight chains cannot hold you down, you must
escape, still fuelled by anger under the midday sun
as rich sounds fill the lively island air.
You plot as Odysseus skips a stone that hops
across the waves, imagining himself skimming
home like a sea-eagle low over the sea,
wide-winged & arrow-fast. You have almost forgotten
how to be generous, kind & decent. Led astray
by lowly masculinity. What will he do now?
He is wedged into the world of men, a place you will
not stay for fear of getting stuck. You are
misunderstood. It's the price you have
paid for hoping that he can change like Dawn, like you.

LEVERS

You're coming back, Calypso, loosening the ties,
these too-tight chains cannot hold you down. You are
escaping, rising to meet yourself in the afternoon sun
as rich sounds fill the lively island air.
You tell Odysseus, as his thick fingers peck
through pebbles, dreaming of skimming
home like a sea-eagle low over the sea,
wide-winged & arrow-fast, you have given
his life back to him twice now. Saved him from the fate
of a lowly mortal. Will he even notice you?
Do you want him to? Think of your escape from them,
back to reign over your kingdom, not like a lowly king, but like
a god & I will consider the price paid in full,
the debt settled, the slate as clean as clouds after rain.

WATER

There you are, Calypso, gift-wrapped by moonlight,
& waiting for the boat to leave, now laden with gifts
to speed his voyage, with charms to protect his little life.
The sound of singing fills the island air & it's yours.
You watch Odysseus as he wields your axe,
notches your planks, drills holes with your gimlet,
stitches his sails with the cloth you wove, his tears dried.
His boat is narrow-hulled & arrow-fast. You have
given his world back to him. Saved him from the fate
of a lowly mortal. Will he even thank you?
You do not need him to. Let him sail
with the pace of the leviathan, fleet of fin.
His crime is having bored me. I consider the price paid,
the debt settled, the slate as clean as the sky after rain.

WINE

There you are, Calypso, gift-wrapped by morning
& waiting for the horizon to clear as shadows
shorten at the edges of your forests, brightening
the rosemary, the jasmine & the cedar-scented cypress.
You wait for Odysseus to disappear, tasting
the salt sea winds. Your footsteps are light with relief
as you turn to home through sunlight & birdsong.
Home. You push aside the vines at your doorway
with a sigh that could draw blossom from trees in spring.
Is that all the hero was, a man who needed help just
to find his way home? & what of you, now alone?
This is more than a home; this is your kingdom.
Perhaps exile is the price you pay for wisdom,
seeing that the ever-hungry men are not enough.

WIND

You are Calypso, still gift-wrapped by this soft light.
Are you waiting for something? For a smudge
on the horizon or a sigh at the vines
around your door? Let my words sting your ears
as if I am Hermes the messenger; you are
not waiting, not watching, not hoping, not trapped.
These are just words men hang about you.
You are in amber here, held safe, separate, apart
but not alone. Your island is full of beauty, enough
to make a god pause. What is a hero now?
Nothing more than a warring monster who wants
to go home, like a small child after a long day
at school, tired, overwhelmed by books & learning.
Experience is the price of wisdom: see how rich we are.

find a place of safety, it could be a
room or a cave, an island, a cliff edge or
a quiet, still place held steady in your
mind's eye and barricade the entrance

bar the windows and if you can, hang wards
and charms across the lintels, be the mad
old bitch that little boys dare each other to
cherry knock, their bright teeth flashing

MELANTHO

ITHACA

There comes a point in most children's lives when they realise that their parents are not superheroes, but ordinary, fallible, maybe not very pleasant people who can't do magic tricks or stop bad things from happening or kiss things better.

There came a point in Melantho's childhood when she realised that her parents had been a wedding gift to the happy couple in the big house from the bride's father.

But it's OK, they didn't wrap them in shiny paper and tie it up with ribbon that someone had curled with the blade of some scissors so that they fell in pretty spirals. They didn't attach a gift tag to them. They didn't do that.

Melantho realised this when her mother was
teaching her how to wash the feet of the man
of the house. She does not remember the
exact exchange, only her confusion, but she
does (fortune be praised!) remember how to
wash a man's feet.

First, you find the shining cauldron. It
must be the shining cauldron, not the
mucky cauldron, the dented cauldron or the
cauldron full of goat's intestines that sits by
the door to the goat shed, a dire warning to
the other goats in regard to their behaviour.

Then you fill the shining cauldron with lots
of cold water and a splash of hot. Carry it
to the man who will be comfortably seated
somewhere chosen for its convenience
to him and not for its proximity to the
extremely heavy cauldron or water source.

Kneel beside the man and think subservient
thoughts, allow these thoughts to shape your
posture while remembering to be comely but
not so comely his wife is offended.

Hold the brave and muscular leg, always
maintain awareness of what an honour this
is. Men cannot wash themselves but it is not
every woman that is chosen to wash them.

Rub the leg with the flat of your palm,
paying careful attention to the amount of
friction, which must be enough to dislodge
dirt but not enough to irritate sensitive and
important skin. Remember that a man has
violent hobbies which may spatter him. Your
feelings about this gore are not important.

Once the man is clean and godlike again,
rub him with oil so that he may return to his
natural habitat as shining as the now filthy
cauldron once was.

You will need also to clean that cauldron so
that you are ready when next summoned.

See the golden boy child who will grow up
to be an unrepentant killer, like his father.
He will be praised for merely coming home,
like his father. He is a chip off the old
block. See him run and shoot and sacrifice
and make plans for his bright future. See
everyone help him carry the terrible burden
of his privilege, ease the load for the poor,
poor boy.

Now see the girl bowed beneath the weight
of that shining cauldron fetching and
carrying and having oily-footed men look
into her face as they hold her by the chin
and calculate how many years, months, days
they ought to wait. This wait becomes a thing
to be grateful for. Like the early morning
when no one else is awake and the air is still
and clean.

Melantho realises, when sewing lessons
start, that there are not many years, months
and days left of relative safety. When you
reach a certain age, you are allowed to sit
with the women and make clothes. Oh, a
blessed life this is!

She is not allowed to use the loom, though.
The gift of weaving is bestowed by a goddess
who does not even see the girls who come
with a label explaining their price at market.
The daughters of Spartan princes have
looms, island demigods have looms. Chattels
do not, they have needles and pins. Sewing is
straightforward and men are not interested
in it or impressed by it, so she is left alone
to pick it up as she goes. One week with
fingertips full of needle pricks and then
she is away, hemming for all of Ithaca. Her
needle flies, it is as fast and sharp as her
tongue has become.

There is another Melantho. She is the Queen of Argos. Perhaps there has been a mix up. Thinking about it, she can really see how much better suited she would be to a life where she didn't face the daily threat of degradation or destitution or devastation. Where she could at least feel better off than someone instead of one rung higher up the ladder than a disembowelled goat. Ah, Argos. Subservient to Sparta, but who isn't. She would rule Argos for five decades.

Our Melantho can only dream of brand-new linen and pitted olives.

Melantho can help in the kitchen now. She can put things in bowls, which are really just smaller, duller cauldrons after all. She can slice some things. What she can't do, because she is a woman and even at the bottom of the pile there is a hierarchy, is anything fancy with meat. Artemis is a woman and she is allowed to hunt but Artemis didn't have wedding presents for parents, she had gods for parents, so she can gallop around forests and fields with a bow and arrow.

Melantho is not even allowed to go to the field next door and bop the nearest sheep on the head. Not that she'd want to. When you have to spend a great deal of time avoiding being bopped on the head yourself, the thought of bopping others, regardless of species, is a distant dream.

Melantho is good at stewing. In all senses of the word.

Now Melantho is older and the chin-holding-and-wondering ritual has been consigned to the past. Unfortunately, she has grown into a woman of the particular shape that is considered attractive, her face has developed in a particular direction thought to be pretty and so she has a great deal of attention bestowed upon her. Men think this attention is a gift, an act of generosity, but actually it is a terror and Melantho considers scalding the very skin from her face if that would mean she'd get a break from it. It would, of course, just make her some sort of novelty conquest, a bet or a dare. Like the maid with one hand or the maid with an eye missing or the maid with no tongue who can't speak, can only make unearthly sounds as if the stars themselves are trying to speak through her.

Fighting back was briefly an option, for about the same amount of time it took to scratch one eye, knee one groin and elbow the back of one head, definitely an option. Her left leg is never the same though, the strange lump of bone protruding from the shin a little where it was broken by repeated kicking and then never given a chance to set properly. It serves as a useful reminder that she is lucky to be alive.

After that it is much easier to play along.
To say the right words, make the right moves
and then when he sleeps siphon off a little
of whatever luxuries he is carrying around
in his manly pockets. The spoils of war, they
call them.

So, when the palace fills up with more
men, bored and waiting and unoccupied,
a number of options present themselves.
Melantho, by now good at the arithmetic
of trauma, decides to become the favourite
of the one who seems the most reasonable
and least foul-smelling. She chooses the
man who designed the plot to kill the golden
boy-child while he was on his little daddy-
finding quest. At least they have an interest
in common.

It is in many ways predictable that the
attributes of most reasonable and least foul-
smelling, as relative virtues, do not prove
comforting. She is not his favourite in the
way that a particular heavy set Molossian
dog is his favourite. The mastiff is fed and
watered as if its diet and nutrition were of
paramount importance. Its collar is polished
as if it were a broadsword. It is not kicked or
punched. And it certainly is not lent to other
men for walks or sport.

This is a place where rape is decriminalised in peacetime and a legitimate weapon in wartime. A place where people, depending on where they were born, cannot participate in democracy by exercising basic voting rights, cannot find enough food to feed themselves, cannot decide what happens to their bodies, cannot rely on the protection of the authorities, cannot find a place of safety, cannot speak up.

Melantho is busying about some battle-
hardened feet when Penelope appears at
the bottom of the staircase which sweeps
dramatically into the hall. The men are
not quite stunned into silence but they do
briefly pause their conversations to leer
in her direction. Penelope explains that
she really must just finish a shroud for
her father-in-law and that only when that
pressing task is finished can she think about
marriage, but she definitely will. Definitely.
Melantho sees this for the cunning tactic it
is. The old man has many years left in him
and is not in desperate need of a shroud.
And Penelope's disgust for her suitors is so
apparent that Melantho would not be unduly
shocked to see Penelope's skin creeping
away across the floor whenever she has sight
or smell of them. The men, of course, read
these signs, these shudders and shivers as
feverish anticipation and if they register
any distress at all they put it down to the fact
that Penelope can only have one of them
and women find making choices nigh on
impossible.

The weeks drag on and Melantho begins to
hear rumours about the shroud. Penelope
is an accomplished weaver and there is
rampant incredulity that it can be taking her
so long to finish. It is, after all, for a man of

average size. Not for a Cyclops. Melantho
finds any excuse to avoid the loom. She
doesn't want to see it, hear it. She expunges
it from her mind. She ignores the incessant
chatter about the shroud as best she can.

The gossip, having run wildly through the
house like a blazing inferno, reaches an
intolerable intensity. Melantho, dragging her
cauldron back to its peg in the storeroom,
passes the kitchen. The servants inside are
consumed by whispers. *She never*, one voice
murmurs. *Honestly*, another hisses, *I saw it
with my own eyes. She was unravelling it. It was
beautiful as well.*

I suspect this will not end well, Melantho
thinks. And these suspicions are confirmed
when that night Penelope sends for her.
Melantho finds herself standing only three
feet from the loom receiving her orders for
the night. The shroud is indeed beautiful,
but not so beautiful that it distracts Melantho
from the gnawing anxiety that now she is
involved. She is an accessory.

Melantho wakes up the next morning
with her neck set in a strange position,
like a distressed swan. She has not been
particularly diligent in guarding the door but
it is locked and bolted. Penelope has clearly
not been disturbed. She is sitting on the end
of her strange tree-bed quite absorbed in her
thoughts as she lovingly unravels the shroud.

It is a complete coincidence that the suitors
discover the secret of the shroud the day
after Melantho spends the night snoring
over the keyhole. But no one will believe that
she hasn't denounced Penelope. Melantho
spends the next few days fending off both
congratulations and contempt. *Better this
than have them think you helped her*, says
her mother. *Better to snitch than to unstitch*,
says Melantho and her mother nods as if
acknowledging great wisdom.

Melantho can hear someone yelling
her name, drunkenness mangling the
enunciation. Life carries on.

Fetch and carry, fetch and carry. That's about
it as far as actual responsibility is concerned.
She got to pour some wine once when one
of the men, dragged into Ithacan servitude
from nobility in Troy, had been stabbed in
the leg for a joke.

As in the suitor who had done it thought
it was a joke, not that the Trojan had told
a bad joke and invited chastisement. He
couldn't tell jokes as they had cut his tongue
out not five miles from the sacked city's
gates, shortly after they'd decided he was not
masculine enough.

LYMNAEA

She could have been a great pond snail.
Great meaning big, rather than excellent.
But she would have been that too. She could
have spent her days gliding upside down
across the surface of the water, not on top
of the water but underneath it. She would
have had a brown spiral shell that would
have protected her from predators and she
would have been a marvellous addition to any
aquarium as she would have kept the tank
clean by eating all the algae and pond scum.

There is a new beggar in court. This one
looks particularly gnarly. He is tied up in rags
like the old corpse of a mangy dog, which is
what he also smells like. He is very tidy with
his fists and has an educated mouth.

Melantho thinks there is a good chance
that he's a god in disguise so, having heard
what happens to young women like her
when gods are in disguise, she decides to
encourage him to leave the palace soon
as and suggests he might be better off in
the smithy, where he won't get kicked and
punched and left for dead.

Like many a god he does not like being told
he looks like a mad old fool and loudly hopes
that the golden boy-child will slice her limb
from limb.

She reflects on this for a moment and,
remembering Medusa in particular, she
concludes that she can cope with being sliced
limb from limb if that's her fate. Rather a
limbless corpse than a living, breathing
cautionary tale for the ages.

Melantho is winding wool for Penelope and
thinking about how if she were Penelope she
would make different choices.

While she does understand that Penelope
can't make as many choices as, say, her
husband or her son, she can make more
choices than Melantho, who can't make any.

Therefore, thinks Melantho, some of the
responsibility must fall on Penelope. With
the ability to decide comes the obligation,
surely, to do so.

And then Penelope smiles at Melantho, even
though her eyes are red from crying and lack
of natural sleep, and she slips the delicate
filigree bracelet from her wrist and gives it
to Melantho.

This is great, Melantho thinks. I will wear
this next time I go to the public square to
hear a poet or to a lavish feast to celebrate
my arrival and status as beloved guest.
She smiles back though and slips it into
her robes.

A little later, Melantho is accused of stealing
the bracelet. Penelope, who has so many
delicate filigree bracelets it is hard to keep
tabs on them all, decides that she is too

consumed with grief to remember her generosity (even though it was only two hours ago).

The possibility of escape is not one Melantho entertains. The thought never occurs because the event never occurs.

Survival? Now, that is worth thinking about.

In fact, Melantho is obsessed with survival.

He comes back, of course, the conquering
hero. Melantho fears she may have backed
the wrong horse when her champion's nipple
is pierced with an arrow and his soul pours
out the hole it leaves.

Her skill with a mop comes in handy. The
shining cauldron can't stand on ceremony
any longer, it must be used to clean the blood
from the walls. She picks a collection of
teeth out from between the flagstones. Her
knees are full of splinters of furniture and
her nostril are full of the smell of iron and
piss and shit. Men are not brave in their last
moments. While she does this, the victors
are celebrating and briefing the poet on what
facts he should include in his epic.

Finally, the last corpse is in the courtyard.
Dawn is announcing the new day. The golden
boy-child grabs her by the hair, not for the
first time, and drags her to a special platform
where she is one of twelve women who are
tied up by the neck and hung. Melantho does
not struggle. She waits until her last breath
and inhales each name of these murdered
women as if this simple act of remembering
will preserve all their lives.

MOIRAI

She could have been the granddaughter of
Prometheus. She could have been of the
lineage that brought flaming civilisation to
dingy humanity.

But she isn't.

She is *this* Melantho. Melantho of the cauldron
and the noose. And she will be heard.

it is no longer necessary that you make
yourself available to them as if you were
not a person but an appointment to be
booked then cancelled at the last minute

&

it is no longer necessary that you hide
your feelings like a child trying to spit
brawny gristle into a tissue at dinner &
smuggle the dampness into her pocket

SCYLLA

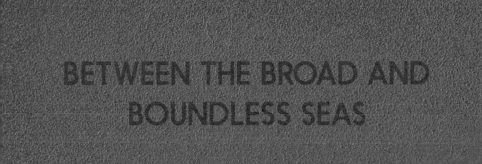

BETWEEN THE BROAD AND
BOUNDLESS SEAS

Way out almost to the land of the dead, past the islands strung like gems across the shot silk of the sea, where two rocks rise out of the water. Each summit is hidden by dolphin-blue fog. No one knows how tall they are, only that the sides are sheer as glass. The channel between them is so narrow no sun can warm it. One side is punctured by a dark hollow gaping over the boundless sea to Hades in a silent howl. This is where Scylla lives.

Ships may pass a little to the left or a little to the right but this choice is merely an illusion. Would you rather be meat or drink?

Shade your eyes and look towards the horizon. There is a ship approaching. With cocky sails billowing it speeds towards the rocks and certain tragedy.

Between the rocks in the damp cold the absence of light takes on a new quality. It becomes the black gape of a pit reaching out to consume whatever has dared to breach its refuge.

They don't see Scylla until she is upon them, all furious teeth and scalding breath. She is too fast for them. They barely have a moment to comprehend the sight. Shock hurls them into benevolent oblivion before her full glory can be witnessed.

They would have seen a titanic figure slithering down the cliffs from the depths of the dark hollow high above them so unrestrained and magnificent she seemed to fill the whole world.

Thoughts (assumed) of the first sailor to be eaten

it's a horde of dogs black as the void pouring dogs made molten and tumultuous the hell-hounds unleashed by Eris herself to devour anything living in their savage sport

Thoughts (assumed) of the second sailor as he
looked up the rock face

it's a whale filthy and diseased the stink of death pouring from it yellowing the air with thick sulphur yet somehow still striving to reach the water before its rotting carcass explodes desperation tearing every sinew and tendon

Thoughts (assumed) of the third sailor
as he saw the first sailor being eaten

what is this a serpent a six-headed eyeless corkscrew of death-snake writhing down to the cliffs with jagged mouths of pyrite teethlike shards of bone kept as souvenirs lumps of stolen flesh nestling against glossy red gums the sickening slither of its scales like a prayer rasping on a final breath

Thoughts (assumed) of the fourth sailor
as he watched the third sailor's legs disappearing

this is a spider dropping through the mist with the heavy weight of gloomy judgment its thorny legs as thick as sequoia trunks threading hanging like drool glistening in the pearl light only death's heralds bring

Thoughts (assumed) of the fifth sailor who plunged
into unconsciousness before the first sailor
had even left the deck

*this crab skittering down the cliff face here its carapace slick with red
has fallen from another earth an impenetrable armour a fortress keeping
nightmares the horror seeping through every crack in the small hours a
craving yearning terror*

Thoughts (assumed) of the sixth sailor

woman
gigantic woman
all of these made monstrous
hounds
whale
serpent
spider
crab
woman
worst
a woman
leaping
towards

And then it really is too late. Nothing more to see. Snapped spine and crushed skull. Ground up. Done, in any case. The scant consolation of an unmarked and empty grave.

They didn't see her before this monstering happened. They didn't see her when she was wreathed in silk and jewels, not yet aware of her story unravelling.

If they had seen her they would have seen a vivid mind and a scorching sense of humour dancing through the bright halls.

But they were too busy plotting, waiting for an opportunity for a spin around the floor, up the stairs, between the sheets.

This nymph, this Scylla, whose is she?
Who lays claim to those eyes, those limbs, that skin?
Who do I steal her away from?

All they saw was a prize to evidence their prowess.

She will do everything for me
she will bring me anything I need
she will do anything I want

I will get what I'm entitled to

All they saw was a payment to settle a debt.

She will make sure I feel cared for
She will make sure I feel loved
She will make sure I feel special
She will make sure I feel strong
She will make sure I feel like a man

All they saw was a mirror to admire themselves in.

I've done it
I am the winner
I have it all
Everything I deserve

All they saw was a trophy to congratulate themselves with.

But then they worried, saw themselves in other men's faces.

What if someone tries to steal her from me
Well, I will lock her away

As if she was a shining hoplon or a pair of particularly fine sandals.

No one seems to have ever wondered

What does Scylla want? What plans is she making? What has she got to say?
Who does she want to be?

Some of Scylla's immediate thoughts
concerning her situation

I do not want to be pursued incessantly by a slimy man who stinks of fish.

I am not planning to spend my life with a slimy man I do not love or want, and who I have explained this to repeatedly.

I find that speaking up is not the problem, fish-stinking dickheads not listening is the problem.

I do not want something awful to happen to me. I do not want to be turned into a monster while I am out bathing. Not because of a misunderstanding between women over a slimy man who stinks of fish unworthy of either of us.

Scylla was poisoned by a rival for a lover she had not had and did not want. The hypocrisy and injustice twisted and buckled her body until a new shape emerged. At first it was just a mass, a pulsing, dull shadow in a dark pit, then a pinpoint of light flashed. Perhaps that was the shine of an eye or the gleam of tooth? Then there was a sound, felt rather than heard, knocking at the solar plexus, deep and resonant. And a rushing. Storm-like. The sense of a tremendous power nearing, nearing until it was upon us, showering sand and pebbles. She grew and grew, terrific, until she was completely transformed. She pulled away, stretching out across the water, onyx scales flashing in the moonlight, the sound of hounds howling filling the air.

It only took a moment but it would never be undone.

So now, six sailors, one for each mouth. Reparations by the half-dozen.

See, though, how she is beautiful out there.
She is beyond the necessity of compromise.
Neither the draft nor the chicken leg can compel her.

She is beyond them, she has escaped.

Their bodies are beneath her contempt.

It takes six of them to satisfy her.

More, sometimes.

Not because she is insatiable but because they are not enough.

When she swallowed each of them whole, not one of them touched the sides.

Ah, the perils of confusing sex and survival.

Scylla is not greedy. Her hunger makes her point with precision and economy.

And those thinking that she will be different for them, tamed for them, would do well to remember this: when the time comes and Heraclean death tries to take Scylla, the sea-gods will make sure that she is reborn in flames.

She will never be their unremembered nymph, bound for the silence of the ocean floor.

She will be as she is now. All her own. Glorious.

just to speak aloud

about anything

together

just to be heard, to hear

loud as a winter carol
chorused in the light
spilling from an opened door

or that joyful yell
of summer toes
feeling the sea
for the first time
in a new year

WOMEN

HADES

The underworld. A place where, ordinarily, people go after their lives are finished. A group of dead women are out walking. It could be a sombre parade or a particularly diffident trip out somewhere everyone has been before. Despite this uninspiring appearance, conversation is both widespread and earnest. Let's listen in.

ORIOLE

Anticleia, mother of Odysseus, and Alcmene, mother of Heracles compare notes.

is that you Anticleia / yes / I couldn't see you through the mist / it is bad today / it is / fog really / yes / time / what for / they say it's time, the mist / really / because time gathers in the Underworld / well

imagine that / yes / I'm breathing in time / you're not breathing you're dead / isn't it amazing what one can get used to / I guess so / I dreaded coming here / me too / Hades

& all of that / I felt the same / heroes eh / you're right Alcmene / who'd have one / you don't choose what you get / no but I wouldn't have chosen a hero / not Heracles? / well / he was a good boy I thought / he was a handful / just

like Odysseus / famous though so I suppose that's / what? / I don't know / go on / I suppose that's something / I would have rather had a farmer-son who stayed at home ploughing / yes / tilling / yes / sowing / they did a lot of sowing / oh you are

awful

CROW

Megara and her aunt, Epicaste, are trying not to catch up to the pair dawdling in front. Megara was Heracles' first wife. Someone will remind us who Epicaste is, someone always does.

there she goes / oh yeah / she's got a nerve / who / Leda / how come / I mean / what? / a swan / I thought it was Zeus / it was, as a swan / these gods / I know but Megara you wouldn't / if it was Zeus / Megara! / what lord of

Olympus? I might / a swan though, nasty creatures / can be beautiful though, Aunt Epicaste / I mean / shush, my mother-in-law is up ahead / which one? / Heracles's mum / oh that one / yes / I thought she was all right / yes she's

all right / a swan though / I feel sorry for her / do you? / everyone knows / do they? / there are pictures of it everywhere / are there / yes even in the future / I mean / we've all got something we're not proud of / I don't / you did marry Oedipus,

your son

EIDER

Here we meet Tyro and Eriphyle. Tyro fell in love with a river-god and Eriphyle started a war because she wanted a necklace. The necklace she so coveted was enchanted and brought bad luck to its wearer. Still, wars have been fought for stranger reasons.

is it colder today / it's always the same temperature / is it / I'm pretty sure / every day / yes / the same / yes / oh Tyro / yes Eriphyle / you are a mine of useful information / just about the weather / & other things, you know the name

of that river / that river? / I can't remember / the one over there? / yes / Cocytus / that's it / river of wailing / so cheerful / this is the Underworld / I know that / realm of the dead / I do know / it's not supposed to be

cheerful / it definitely isn't that / no it's a bit maudlin / yes / (long silence) / what's that river called again? / right over there / yes / Lethe / what's that the river of / forgetfulness I think / I couldn't remember / what? / sorry very

bad joke

CARDINAL

Ariadne, half-sister of the minotaur, and Phaedra step out for a breath of not-air. Phaedra married Theseus, who had just abandoned her sister Ariadne, who had helped him kill that minotaur. But to be fair, or maybe just incredulous, Theseus did kidnap Phaedra, so...

(silence) / (no reply) / (Ariadne sighs) / (silence) / (no reply) / (awkward pause) / (another sigh) / (Phaedra steps carefully over a clavicle) / (sniff) / (silence) / (sniff) / (silence) / (blows nose) / (checks to see if Ariadne is crying) / (she

isn't)

RAIL

Anticleia and Alcmene pass by again. There is no information on who they had stopped to talk to, who the 'she' they are referring to is. It isn't me.

she was nice / I thought so / I like it when people stop to talk / people round here don't much / they're too busy being ephemeral I expect / it's very fashionable / rather too much wafting / I agree / it's incredible what speed

some of them can get up to / I know / this morning / when's morning / I mean earlier then / go on / I saw Procris and Clymene and Alcmene / who? / never mind, they were wafting / and Antiope / oh that one's always wafting / still Iphimedeia is nice / is

that her name? / yes / isn't she the one / what? / who / what? / you mean who / what? / the one who / tell me / what? / stop that, just tell me about Iphimedeia / I was just going to say that she's the one who had

twins / lots of people have twins / not like these ones / how so? / they were nine fathoms tall / that is tall / and nine cubits round the chest / they were huge / I know / imagine the pain / of what? / of giving in birth to them / no they were normal until age

nine

CRAKE

There are a number of Maeras in Greek mythology, and at this point our Maera is wondering which one she might be. She is walking alone. Talking to oneself is a suspicious act in the Underworld too. Or maybe she is walking in a group of selves. It's almost impossible to say.

are we any nearer Maera no not any nearer I'm afraid to what to working out who we are we I mean I not we who I am I'm sorry bad habit I think today I feel more like the daughter of Atlas than of a river-god anyway definitely not a

hound

JAEGER

Ah, Phaedra and Ariadne have come back and they appear to be talking now.

Ariadne / what? / this is a bit silly / what is? / us not talking / I quite like it / but we're going to be here for all eternity / yes / so we might as well have a chat once in a while / to pass the time / if you like / the Underworld is

enormous / seems like it / so why don't you go to a different bit? / I like this bit near the Asphodel / you would / what's that supposed to mean / they're miserable flowers / they're pretty / they're not / in their own way / like

you I suppose / well if you're going to be insulting / (sniff) / and you ran off with my husband so / he ran off with me, literally / you helped / yes but then he left me and I ended up here so it's not really all that romantic

and lovely / I never said it was / you implied it / I didn't / you did / I'm well aware of what Theseus was like / I wasn't / that's the problem with heroes / what is? / I guess on the whole they're just not very

nice

NIGHT-HERON

Megara and Epicaste have paused nearby. Let their voices now travel into our ears as if by accident, without us making any effort to listen (that would be eavesdropping – a poor habit).

I think the problem is that we excuse them / who? / husbands and sons Megara / I think I've lost the thread here Aunt / I was thinking out loud really / I'm listening / I mean / we excuse them? / yes / who? / heroes / I'm not sure that

your son slash husband was a hero / tragic hero I think / really? / he did suffer / he had mental health problems I think you'll find / that's suffering / yes but not in / what? / nothing, it doesn't matter / what's wrong? / don't you get

bored? / of what? / talking about them all the time / what else is there to do / look at Phaedra and Ariadne over there / yes / they'll be talking about Theseus / at least they're talking about something and not just

arguing

STORM-PETREL

Tyro and Eriphyle are still chattering away, but not about bodies of water or jewellery.

did you like Penelope? / what made you think of that suddenly? / Megara over there / yes / used to be married to Heracles / well? / I like her, very reasonable woman / I see / what about Penelope? / very pretty / yes / very wealthy

family / that's important / I didn't think she'd like it on Ithaca / no? / it's just a rock in the middle of the sea / right / it's a nice home for goats / oh / I can't think of a woman less like a goat than

Penelope / good at weaving / a keen weaver / obsessive / an obsessive weaver / aren't we all darling / I'm not / no I never saw the appeal to be honest / the gods love it / they've got too much time on their

hands

RAVEN

Maera lollops by with her tongue hanging out and her tail wagging, and I wonder what smells there are for a hound to chase in the Underworld. Probably none. I also wonder whether she would be better approaching her afterlife as a sea-nymph. And I say that as a dog person.

I don't mind what don't you mind being the hound I like dogs I'm not sure a hound is the same as a dog & anyway I mind do you yes I mind very much why well because no one knows who I am & they're all too

embarrassed to talk to me even though they're no better really I know what their problem is do you yes I do too woof shut up howl shush now what's the problem it's because you don't have any children maybe I'll have

some puppies don't be like that they all think they're better than me growl yap stop it they don't you think they're better than you you're the daughter of a titan & the daughter of a god & a nymph oh yeah & a lover of

Zeus that's not unusual yes so it's better to be one than not be one isn't it it's a bit like all those Thebans like Chloris having the same handbag or the hounds of Hades all having three heads why must we always come back to the

hounds

QUELEA

We cannot help but overhear what Tyro and Eriphyle are saying. I didn't mention before, it's not really for me to bring up, but Eriphyle did take the necklace in return for persuading her husband to fight a battle in which he was killed. Ah, well.

I need to ask you something / go on / how much? / what? / how much gold? / I see / now don't be like that / like what? / I just want to know how much Eriphyle / how much gold? / yes / how much gold I got for

my husband? / yes / a surprisingly large amount given what a fucking useless bastard he was / was he? / terrible in bed / really / never turned into any kind of animal didn't like the water pouring through my

lap trick / they love that / I know, not him though / bit vanilla / oh dear, mind you / what? / mine were all like that / really? / I think it's a myth / what is? / all that leaping in & out of bed changing shape & using / using what? / all that

equipment / Tyro! / well people do gossip don't they / don't they though / you hear things / you do? / mind you sometimes I'd rather not / what? / hear things / what you do mean? / like you / me? / & the twins / the

twins? / you don't have to talk about it / I'm not / I mean I'm sure you had your reasons / their father / what? / their father / yes / it was him or them & you know how they are when it's like that he always comes

first / (snorts) / anyway that's one of the things I like about it down here / what? / how they all stay away, the heroes / they're doing their re-enactment thing over in Elysium / what are they re-enacting? / Troy I expect / still it's only a matter of time / what is? / we haven't had a visitation for a while / that's true / who was it last time? / that Orpheus / no that was the time before / was it? / yes / the other one beginning with O / Odysseus? / that's it / Anticleia was

surprised

here we are, we are sisters now
scattered on different islands but
steady before our looms, shuttles
chattering, revealing our designs
this is a community of sorts
or perhaps a secret society
the quiet signals singing across oceans
gathering, gathering, gathering

CIRCE

AEAEA

OLEANDER

Circe, what is this island if not an idyll,
a home for you, far away, distant & protective?
Your wild-hearted woods, tumbling into the shore's sandy coves,
are a place of safety, haven for the creatures in your care.
These lions & wolves, once savage with hunger,
blood-stained, starved to the bone, now roam a kinder kingdom,
the air alive with the singing of your voice & loom,
another weaver at this women's work, spinning spells & stitches.
Your emerald forests have shared their secrets with you,
until your magic has filled these acres of wilderness
from your sky-bearing mountains to the coast-breaching seas.
These island days are meant for remembering, pausing,
winding a stopped clock whose chime is seldom heard.
Send out your bright story, set it to rest lightly in the world.

ROSARY PEA

Circe, what is this island if not a prison,
a cage for you, cast away, disowned & denied?
Your night-stained woods, banked hard against the shore's bladed edge,
are a meeting place, shelter for the invaders at your gate.
These men the sea delivers, still savage with war,
blood-drenched down to the bone, steeped in murder,
swamp your villa with their appetites, all gluttonous
entitlement, your halls ring with the singing of swords.
Yet these dark forests would share their lessons with you
until your incantations fill the ears of men
from the sky-bearing mountains to the coast-breaching seas.
But still fear loiters along the horizon like
a ship-swallowing fog, darker than any small hour.
Send them your bright spell, launch its light into the wind.

DEADLY NIGHTSHADE

Circe, what is this island if not a question,
a puzzle for you, left alone, defiant & resolved?
Your night-stained rooms, cloaked in shade beneath violet skies
are a hiding place, sanctuary from the invaders at your table.
Run. These men the battlefield called to are courting violence,
rage-scorched, burnt through to the soul, coursing with poison.
They ruin your villa with their want, now hateful,
seduced by murder, loving the privilege of war.
How these dark times coax your hard lessons from you
& your incantations fill the winds
from the sky-bearing mountains to the coast-breaching seas.
Now an idea comes, waiting beyond the horizon to
scatter the night like dawn, stronger than any blood vow.
Send them your bright spell, launch its light into the wind.

WHITE SNAKEROOT

Circe, what is this island if not an answer,
a puzzle solved, unravelled, untangled, untied?
Your night-stained skin, cloaked in shade beneath violet skies,
is a patient curse, calamity for the invaders by your bed.
See these murderers as animals, made mad with violence,
no longer human, no longer men, already begging for poison
to still their hands, quiet these restless limbs, to stop
this raging blood, to loosen the heavy chains of war.
How these blind fools demand hard lessons from you
& your incantations colour the lives of men,
because your time-stilling grief will unwind your tongue.
Soon the end will come, arrowing over the horizon
like a bird of prey, intent on a particular target.
Send them your bright spell, launch its light into the wind.

CASTOR BEAN

Circe, what is this island if not a shelter,
a home for you, safe, sound, far out of reach?
Your pinpoint mind, leaning dark towards cool revenge,
is a patient curse, a promise for the invaders by your bed.
& now these animals begin to change, writhe in violence,
at once terrified & horrified, already begging for mercy
with the last dying sounds of vowels & consonants.
Their pitiful squeals fall on uncaring ears, a sigh in a tornado.
Yet still these blind fools will not stay away from you
although your incantations steal the lives of men
& your world-burning rage will unleash your tongue.
So, now the end will come, arrowing over the horizon
like a bird of prey, intent on a particular outcome.
Send them your bright spell, launch its light into the wind.

WATER HEMLOCK

Circe, what is this island if not yours alone,
a territory for you to forge from iron earth?
Your pinpoint mind, leaning dark towards cool revenge,
is a patient curse, a promise to the invaders by your bed.
& now these animals hold no sway, can't threaten violence,
no longer terrify or horrify, already begging for poison.
You will still their hands, quiet restless limbs, to stop
their pitiful squeals, remind them of the price of war.
Yet still these blind fools will not stay away from you
& your incantations colour the lives of men,
because your world-burning rage will unleash your tongue.
So now an end must come, arrowing over the horizon
Like a bird of prey, intent on a particular outcome.
Send them your bright spell, launch its light into the wind.

CAPE LILAC

Circe, what is this island if not a shelter,
a home for you, safe, sound, far out of reach?
Your pinpoint mind, leaning dark towards cool revenge,
is a fate worse than death for unsuspecting men.
& so as pigs they test their snouts against the earth,
uprooting soil & stones, searching for acorns & bugs.
Hauling rounded bellies inches above the mud, they
squint into the bleached sky, their memories stirring.
They cannot fathom why this has befallen them,
what possible fault or failure made forfeit their human form.
Because your world-burning rage can remake them, knit their
bones into new forms, new shapes, reveal them as clearly
as a ship-saving lighthouse, showing a path from present danger.
Send them your bright spell, launch its light into the wind.

MOUNTAIN ARNICA

Circe, what is this pen if not an illustration,
a perfect rendering of what you've always known?
Or perhaps a warning to those heedless fools
who mistake your lustre, accept only face value?
Who will see beyond the nymph with lovely braids?
Who will tremble, not with excitement, but with blank
horror, too late to realise you can make a noose
of those braids as your scalpel tongue cuts free the truth.
Your lions pace among the wolves. Their roars shaking
the island's roots, the piggies squeal & snuffle until
the pride yawns & settles down to sleep. How tedious
these men were, how predictable. They are a little
more appealing now, trotters deep in mud, snouts rustling in swill.
Spare them your bright self, save your light for something else.

WOLFSBANE

Circe, what is this fight if not a fix?
What are their rules if not weighted against you,
& your sister-nymph, Scylla, her monstering your shame?
She is better off, abjected, outside the ring
beyond their gloves. You, honed as their weapon, have followed
& now your handiwork is as infamous as hers.
But still these blind fools will not heed the warning
that your incantations steal the lives of mortal men.
How far must you go until they hear you, see you?
Will it be when every foot is trottered, every nose a snout?
Trust that your world-shaping words will reclaim your life
& for now wait, hold yourself tall & steady like
a pillar of smoke rising upright in the still cold air.
Send me your bright spell, launch its light into the world.

THIMBLEWEED

Circe, what is your name if not a spell
to conjure metamorphoses worthy of a god,
declaimed like a prayer in a time of crisis,
lark song in the early morning, summoning
the clear light of dawn so time can start over.
So we can start over, begin again with all
the wisdom of experience & exile held high,
a standard raised. Circe, your name is a charm.
Power is not a comfort, a rocking chair
set on a porch to sit & watch the moon rising.
How much easier to have potential, to rest
before the endeavour, like planning a long climb
as the weather breaks. It is too late now, you have arrived.
Send me your bright spell, launch its light into the world.

ANTHURIUM

Circe, what is your name if not a spell,
whispered like the kingfisher's wing at the water's edge?
A flash of electric blue seen too late from the
corner of my eye, & then that sense of being
lucky & unlucky simultaneously,
to have missed & caught in the same scant moment.
But at least I have tried to see, tried to recognise
those things that stay hidden, submerged below the line.
What comfort is there in being seen but not
recognised? You are representative,
a symbol, a cipher. Always less than an immortal.
Why care then? Your exile is their banishment,
their punishment. It is they who you will forget.
This is your bright spell, set it to rest lightly in the world.

COLUMBINE

Circe, what is your name if not a spell,
murmured like the north wind at a loose latch or
else sung like a bell tolling a baleful warning.
Is a lesson taught too late any lesson at all?
& what is truth? I might say it's the words of someone
trusting of love. Circe, if you cast your spell upon
not a man, not a pig, but yourself, what would you be?
A phoenix, ash-tipped wings stretched above the cliff
or a monster, a livid corpse of festered dreams & mildewed hopes?
Set them free, return them, they are not worth your words,
even though they will think they won. Let them go
& sit with me as I set in sonnet these island days as if
winding a stopped clock whose chime is long forgotten.
This is your bright spell, set it to rest lightly in the world.

MARSH MARIGOLD

Circe, what is this pen if not a commemoration?
Here are these bristling trophies, won with art & guile,
a credit to your knowledge of herbs & potions,
to your bravery & cunning. These pigs rootle in
slurry & swill with snouts & trotters instead of
their fists & tongues, stinking more, if possible,
squealing more, if possible. Send them away from here.
Free yourself from this dull responsibility,
they are not worthy of your continuing attention.
These men the battlefield clung to now cry & fuss,
new fear shifts restless along the horizon like
a ship-swallowing serpent, keener than any taut bow.
Release them to tell their tale of cruel mistresses but
send me your bright spell, launch its light into the world.

MANDRAKE

Circe, what is an island if not a realm,
a kingdom for you to rule, like a king but just?
Your ancient spell revealing hidden truths for all to see
is a lesson taught too late for men who never learn.
& what of you, will you test your soul against your form,
stare into the bleached sky, searching for answers & escape?
Will I? Could we, together, reveal the hidden truth or only
wrap ourselves in elaborate disguises? Send them away from here.
Consign these men to the Underworld, like the dead
& ended, show them the future. Give them one more
chance if that's what you want, if that's what hope does.
I am not so hopeful. I think the time for looking
back is done, for salt in wounds, for listening. All done.
Send me your bright story, set it to rest lightly in the world.

LARKSPUR

Circe, what is this island if not an idyll,
a home for you once again, distant & protective?
Your soul-flighting songs, sounding at the shore's farthest reaches,
are a charm of safety, a prayer for the creatures in your care.
You are at home again, once savage & raging,
fear-soaked, wearied to the bone, now you can roam your
kingdom, following no man's rules or reasoning, just
another weaver at your own life's work, spinning spells.
Keep on, keep on, your shuttle flying in & out
until your cloth has filled up acres of such wildness
you can only be glimpsed like the flash of colour in shot silk.
Your island days are meant for retelling, wondering,
winding a stopped clock whose chime is seldom heard.
Send out your bright story, set it to rest lightly in the world.

MEADOW SAFFRON

Circe, what is a story if not a necessity,
a meditation on unaskable questions?
What if you cast your spell on not an island, not a soldier,
but on a jury, on a parliament,
on a producer, on a singer-songwriter?
You could make a farmyard of our four estates,
or worse, expose this gaping hellmouth, their fetid
terror metastasised into stuttering impotent hate.
This island is all their own, sheering away
into the freezing dark maw, dragging us with them.
A hero is merely a man who finds his way home,
& that is their bar, set so low we trip over it.
Circe, step around it, swerve, sashay & I will
send out your bright story, set it to rest at odds with the world.

pray silence for the goddess

there is nothing she dare say
surely, not now the judges must
themselves be spotless

we are all grimy with
mistakes, all of us

like a filthy dog, dying by the
side of the road

fatally wounded by exhaustion

ATHENA

THE BLINK OF AN EYE

Athena finds it hard to make friends. Other children's words fall on her ears like ash from a volcano suffocating a small hillside village.

In the playground she stands on the edge of their games as if populating the overlapping centre of a Venn diagram. The part labelled 'lonely'.

In the classroom she sits halfway between the front and the back, very still with her palms pressed against the underside of her desk so that she won't raise her hand by mistake. She concentrates on the feeling of the cool wood and that way makes herself invisible.

When she is invisible she wanders off somewhere else. Out through the window and over the olive groves to the barren mountainsides where the sun beats down, pushing the weeds back into the stony earth. She sees everything because no one sees her.

No one sees her even when she isn't invisible, because she arrives in places they don't expect her. She can walk right up to someone and sing a rude song her half-sister has taught her into their face and they don't react. She doesn't do that very often though because the rude song makes her insides feel like they are sweating and all her organs are sliding around in the slickness.

Athena can make herself look like different people and animals. Her stepmother tells her never to make herself look like a bucket or a tree, something without a brain or a mouth, as she won't be able to turn herself back.

You are such a headache, her stepmother says. Or, Go away I have a headache. Or, Your presence is oppressive, I think it might set off one of my headaches. And then her handmaidens laugh behind their hands as if that will catch all the sound and Athena will not hear them.

Athena finds it hard to make friends. Other people's laughter falls on her ears like shrapnel from an explosion tearing through a seaside resort.

Athena makes herself look like an owl. She likes owls. She has a story book with an owl on the cover and the owl has glasses on and a bow tie. His chest feathers are patterned to look like argyle socks and he has bottle-green spatterdashes on his feet, his yellow claws poking out beneath. She doesn't look like that owl, though, she looks like an elf owl. She is the size of a sparrow with grey feathers. Her yellow eyes are framed by white eyebrows which make her look surprised. Displeased. She likes to fly over the olive groves and across the mountains to the treeline where she can sit and watch the moon sinking into the sea, reaching out a last finger across the water towards her.

I see you, the moon says.

Athena worries that she isn't destined for great things, that her father will rue the day she leapt out of his head.

He talks a lot about rueing the day. According to him it is mostly other people that will be doing the rueing but some day he will rue the day and it will be because of Athena leaping out of his head.

One of her many half-brothers told her that when she was born their uncle Helios almost fell out of his chariot and the sun paused in the sky. He said this was because she was so hideous but one of her handmaidens had said it was because she was beautiful. And to stay away from Helios and Hephaestus. And Helios wasn't an uncle, he was more of a close family friend. It was also because instead of being born the normal way she had leapt out of their father's head which was unheard of.

Athena does not find herself beautiful but sometimes she turns herself into someone beautiful just to see what it's like.

Athena makes herself look like the best friend of Nausicaa, princess of Phaeacia. People like beautiful people, particularly women. And Athena wants to be liked by people, particularly women.

At first she visits in the night, while Nausicaa sleeps. She slips through the keyhole like the scent of valerian and sits on the edge of Nausicaa's bed watching the dreams tremble against her eyelids.

Later she visits in the early morning, claiming
she is returning from the harbour having waved
goodbye to her sea-captain father. She helps
to pick flowers and swims in clear water,
marvelling at her body moving beneath the
surface. They laugh and sing until the real
sailor's daughter appears.

Later still she returns one last time to exhort
Nausicaa into doing some laundry so she can
rescue a man and provide him with clothing, lest
he be stranded, naked, down by the river forever.
Nausicaa thinks Athena is a dream.

Athena finds it hard to make friends. Other people's
pity falls on her ears, no longer like ash but like
more snow falling, deepening the drifts that cut off
mountain towns from society.

Athena is not fond of sheep. It's the oblong
pupils that put her off. She feels similarly about
goats. It's also the smell, and the oily yet waxy
feel of their wool.

She is early for their appointment. He is still
asleep under the tree where they left him with all
his Phaeacian treasure piled up around him, so
it looks like a dragon's lair al fresco. More spoils
than if he had returned from the Trojan War on
time. Like a cat landing poised on all four paws.
He didn't know they had an appointment. He
never knew.

Instead of going to wake him up she has decided
to take a walk down from the fields on the rocky
hillside above the town, killing time. She has a
lot of time. She has all the time in all the worlds.
Her time is timeless. It is simultaneous.

The fields are not the lush green fields of Aeaea
where Circe finds her ingredients, or the red
fields of Erytheia where Geryon rears red cattle.
These are grey fields. All flint and granite poised
to avalanche towards the sea. Like cliffs that
have been dislodged by a terrific gust of wind. Or
toppled gravestones. The sheep's hooves clatter
over the stones as they follow the path between
the gorse and thistles. Athena likes the speckles
of yellow from the heads of the gorse and the
lavender prickles of thistle, highlights among the

grey rock and the dirty white sheep and her own brown shepherding robes.

Why don't I have a dog, Athena thinks. That would have been nice, walking along with a dog by my side. No, she thinks, a dog would worry the sheep.

She crests a hill and stops, the sheep milling around as she looks out over the eastern side of the island. She can see his house and land, and then his father's house and land, then beyond, tumbling down towards the harbour, the town. The people are hurrying about the narrow streets, clambering up and down the steps between the small white buildings, blue doors opening and closing, opening and closing.

He is still sleeping. If Athena looks hard she can see him as if he were no more than eight feet away. She can hear him snoring like a pig stuck in a trough. Why are they never glamourous? I suppose because they age, she thinks. Still, he can look however she wants him to. She could take years off him, add them on. She could make him taller, younger, stronger. She could make him do whatever she wanted, pretty much.

She is paralysed by the possibilities.

A sheep, those fiendish oblong pupils glinting in the sunlight, noses her hand. Its muzzle is soft and warm, its gentle breath in her hand is inoffensive.

Which one are you? Athena says. There is always
the possibility that an animal or a tree is a woman
she once knew, a nymph often, sometimes a
mortal. Metamorphosis or unwanted pregnancy;
two career choices for pretty girls. And there are
so many pretty girls, she thinks. Athena thinks
all girls are pretty in one way or another. She
stands on a ridge above a town full of pretty girls
as they go about their business in differing states
of obliviousness.

None more pretty than Penelope, although she is
facing a slightly different horror. Same species,
different creature, thinks Athena. Like the
sheep on Ithaca and the sheep on Sparta where
Penelope came from. The sheep on Sparta have
four legs the same length because they don't have
to spend all their time walking around the same
steep hill in the same direction trying not to
slip down into the sea. The sheep in Ithaca have
adapted to living on the wonk.

Penelope has a house full of monsters who would
marry her before doing… things that Athena
won't allow to graphically flood her mind. I do,
Penelope would say. You do what though? You do
acknowledge any lack of choice in the matter?

Athena reminds herself of the body she is in,
that it is male, and these concerns evaporate. She
contemplates turning into an owl or sending a
cold fog down the hills to shroud the town, just to
remind herself who she is really, just to remind

herself that she isn't subject to these... what?
Realities. She is not subject to any reality. Not even
the reality of time. Or gravity.

The friendly sheep totters away down the hill
leaving droppings behind as it goes, like black
olives. You could be Ares in a better world,
Athena says, if I could make the world. The limits
of power are frustrating wherever they lie.

A strange mist rolls in from the sea. A mist of
overlooking, of not noticing. It shrouds the island.
Athena approves of her handiwork and wanders
down the path that leads through the fields
towards the sea. She skirts the town and leaves her
sheep, or someone's sheep, in a field stippled with
rough tufts of grass.

He is awake and counting his riches. But then
he starts to pace back and forth in the lapping
waves, as he is wont to do.

And then he bursts into tears. As he is wont to
do also.

Athena wonders if the stone ship has made
it back to Phaeacia yet, if the people have
started their fervent prayers to try to provoke
Poseidon's mercy.

Cheer up love, it might never happen,
Athena says.

He is delighted to see another human. He has no idea where he is or how he will carry his treasure home. He remains as clueless as ever. His effusive greeting is comforting, like that of a dog after you've left it home alone for an hour or two and it has spent the time convincing itself that you are dead.

He doesn't know where he is and pretends to be someone different. From Crete or some nonsense.

Athena, bored by him, takes her immortal form. Oh, he says. It's you. She detects a note of disappointment in his voice, as if he would rather shoot the breeze with a shepherd for a while.

She surrounds him with a fine mist so he can walk home without anyone having to be bothered by him. She misses Perseus sometimes. At least he slayed monsters. And he invented quoits.

Maybe after I've sorted all this out, she thinks, I'll go and have a nice game of quoits. With some friends.

MENTES

Athena stops at the gate and adjusts her beard. She can't remember how long Mentes' beard has become and although none of these idiots will remember the real Mentes, she is a perfectionist and so these details are important.

No one in their right mind would enter the courtyard dressed as a woman, no one. The only women inside, Athena knows, are slaves. And Penelope. She isn't a slave, she isn't subjected to that particular horror. She is instead described as eligible.

Athena, being a god, is sympathetic to the idea of hierarchies, the hierarchy of pain being a particular favourite. She has adjudged Penelope's distress dismissible when compared to the pain of, say, Eurycleia.

She pushes the gate open and a wall of odour snatches at her breath. She can smell smoke and hot animal fat and blood, heavy like a clenched fist. Then comes the noise; a chorus of gossip and boasting broadcast for the sole benefit of the speaker. It is a wonder they have not murdered each other by now, she thinks.

She finds a chair covered with cow hide and only the vaguest of stains, and slumps into it, her bronze spear propped against her leg. There is a girl poking the fire with a sword. The sword has a kink in it as if someone has used it as a blunt instrument and simply smashed another person on the head with it. Athena rustles up a carafe of honeyed wine and the leg of something charred beyond recognition out of fresh air, so that no one will have to bring her anything or wash her feet or fear her intentions.

The men all look the same to her. Like ham hanging in the hot window of a charcuterie surrounded by sweaty cheeses and unspeakable jams. She looks around for the boy-child. She supposes he is more of a man now, but he's done little more than sit around fretting and moaning like an ailing bovine. That would pass for a man around here though. It wasn't like this in Heracles' day, Athena sighs.

One of the men nearby pulls a girl down onto his lap and she wriggles about trying to get up and the group of men surrounding them laugh as if this is hilarious. Then the girl starts to laugh too, having quelled her natural instincts enough to focus on surviving at least for the next ten minutes. Athena barely flickers an eyelid and the man expends all his talent before even getting his chiton under control. The girl slips away. Everyone laughs except the prematurely spent hero, who pulls a knife from his sandal strapping and stabs it into the arm of his chair. He manages a laugh then.

Where is the boy? She looks around. Maybe she will have to summon him. It's so dull having to do everything for them. As if she has nothing better to do. She fluffs out the bottom of her beard. It is an extremely paternal beard. She wonders if she should have worn the purple cloak, then she would have been more noticeable. It was very poor form to leave a stranger unacknowledged for this long. Particularly an honoured guest-friend of the homeowner.

She looks around for Mentor, her near-namesake. He interests her. Ah, there he is. He is chewing his bottom lip and furrowing his brow intently. He has the look of a man whose conscience is telling him to speak up and protest. A man who is desperately trying to wait it out until his conscience gives in. He is like that little white ball skittering around the roulette wheel.

Athena hears a voice in her ear. Good evening stranger, and welcome. Come share our dinner. It is the boy. Athena clambers geriatrically to her feet and follows him into the house proper.

As young people tend to do with old people, he parks her on another chair, this one with an embroidered covering and a footstool. It is a little more refined inside than outside but not much. There are a lot of girls busying about. There is food and drink everywhere. Athena almost leans in and asks him if he thinks that maybe people would stop eating him out of house and home if he stopped serving it to them in golden bowls and cups. What good would it do, she thinks.

He wants to know about his father. His mind is a
set of empty bookshelves waiting to be filled with
volume after volume of instruction manuals,
adventure stories and family sagas. How like a
child you are, Athena thinks. Haven't you grown
she says, quite the dowager aunt behind the
beard and the penis. He frowns.

So, your father is alive and stuck on an island.
She leaves out the bit about the beautiful
woman. Men, especially the young ones, tend to
misunderstand the concept. She dares to make
a prophecy that his father will soon return. The
boy looks at her with big wet eyes like a fawn, or
like the nymph the fawn probably once was.

Why are they so incompetent, she thinks, or
rather why am I constantly surprised by it? She
sighs and pulls the boy nearer so she can pour
instruction into his ear.

Twenty oars, remember, she says. Twenty.
There'll need to be an even number of oars on
both sides, or you'll just go round and round. His
eyes look slightly glazed, the bookshelves in his
mind creaking under the sudden weight. It will
take something showy and decisive to spur him
into action. The poor boy has not had a father for
so long fatherly advice is less compelling that it
might have been.

Athena surrounds them both with smoke and
flies up into the rafters as if she is a bird or

the last black gasp of smoke from a spluttering candle. The boy gapes after her and then pulls himself together.

Athena sits in the rafters for a bit listening to the poet singing about how Athena herself had cursed the journey of the Greeks sailing home from Troy. As usual, there is no attempt to relay the facts and the narrative makes no sense at all. Not given how she'd sponsored the Greeks, even to the extent of sanctioning the mass rape of Trojan women, and given how it was Poseidon who had cursed their journey because they'd blinded his son, her cousin.

That is the problem with the Cyclops though, they are twice as easy to blind as anyone else.

And now, inevitably, there is bloodshed.

The finest young man in all of Ithaca, another liar
and thief, a rapist, a murderous killer, holds aloft
his wine glass, savouring its scent and lustre, but
as he begins to lift it to sip an arrow punctures
his carotid and he feels the blood soak his
chiton. He kicks out, looking to gain a foothold
in this world, but as the food and drink scatters
so too does his life.

Athena in the rafters looks down laser-eyed on
the battle below. It is more of a skirmish but
she can see a poet hiding behind an upset table
so it will become a battle when he tells the tale
later. The poets are always spared. Nasty little
creatures.

Athena is assailed by the iron tang of fresh
blood, fetid with flavours of an abattoir. For
her, death has become a rolling conveyor belt of
other people's downfalls. Some pointless, others
grandiose.

The skirmish bears few of Athena's trademarks. It
is more characteristic of the raw brutality of Ares'
wars, enacted for the love of destruction, for the
sake of destruction.

She knows she is kidding herself. She is no
better than Ares. Cleverer, perhaps. Better at
statecraft. But the lives of others seep away just

as cheaply through gaps between flagstones as
they do through the dirt of the battlefield.

Unable to remain uncelebrated anymore,
the returning, all-conquering hero reveals
himself and the suitors, predictable and
unimaginative, wheel away like startled horses
in a thunderstorm. And now there is strategic
thought in evidence. Just a little, for a moment.
The hero and his tiny band take up their position
in a doorway and trap the horde of suitors in a
small space, like an amphora full of wasps.

Another liar and thief, a rapist, a murderous
killer leaps to his feet and emits a pathetic battle
cry that would chill the very souls of tiny babies
and nervous grandparents. His heart is no longer
in it. He is felled by an arrow to the nipple,
smashes headfirst into a table and spills his
brains across the floor.

Athena wonders if she should go down, put in an
appearance so the poet knows to mention her.
She ought to do something, but she is not
feeling herself.

The next liar and thief, rapist and murderous
killer sees the tip of a spear appear through
his chest and he is surprised by this; in all the
clamour he had not heard anyone creeping up
behind him, their spear cocked and ready to
thrust. A man like him is unaccustomed to these
things. Rarely is a life like his punctuated by his

own pain. But now he too has succumbed to this
war in miniature.

The priest is not spared. Only his clothes are
priestly, beneath them he is just like the others.
They are all ended easily by the blade of a
sword slicing from ear to opposing shoulder,
head cleanly falling down, coming to rest near
the lifeless foot of someone now forgotten,
celebrated only by idiots.

Athena is obligated somehow to this scene
although she can't think how or why. Which one
thing led to this other? Lately, time has been
snagging her thoughts, like a torn fingernail on
a silk sleeve. How did I get here? Why is this
happening? She's never thought these things
before but now all that time is splintering, all
that immortal space breaking off. One jagged
sliver after another.

There aren't many left now, the room is clearing,
but there is another liar and thief, a rapist, a
murderous killer trying to push a sword back
into his thigh. He has pulled it out a little, just
a little, and seeing the blood fountain from the
widening wound he panics and tries to nurse the
sword back like a cork into a half-drunk flagon.
No one will help him. Everyone is too busy trying
to save themselves from a similar misfortune.

Athena could save him but if she saves him she
would have to save everyone and she can't save
everyone. No one can.

Hold on.

She can't save everyone. Is that how it works? She doesn't feel sure anymore. Perhaps everyone can be saved. People expect their gods to be certain, Athena thinks, don't they? So, she becomes certain she can't save everyone. Many of them are dead already.

What is happening to me, Athena thinks, what is happening? Who has got hold of me?

Enough.

Athena steps down through metres of nothing to the floor below. It is slick with death. She lifts her aegis high and the liars and thieves, rapists and murderous killers that are still shifting air through their cursed lungs trample each other in their last attempt to break free. She is caught by the repeating details. Tiny emblems. The ragged, glistening edges of fatal wounds and the panting terror of final breath attempting to form prayer.

Number saved: none. Their relatives will collect their bodies from the haphazard piles in the courtyard later, when word has spread.

The poet's work begins immediately.

Athena does not stay for the ritual slaughter of the twelve girls who have done nothing wrong except survive this long, against all hope and expectation. She thinks of them, just for a moment, before the mists close around her. She forces herself to pay attention. There is a single neck snapping in extreme close-up. The noise of it like a startled voice. A young girl's high pitch, speaking no words, just sounding a single exclamation mark.

Soon, inevitably, there will be more bloodshed. But not on Ithaca. She is tired of it so they will have to stop. At least for a short time.

ARACHNE

Athena is working at her loom. Centuries of practise showing in the sureness of her hands. The shuttle seems to pass back and forth between them under its own volition, slipping under the threads as easily as the breeze. The fabric, patterned to mimic the sunlight playing on the sand in the shallows of an Aeaean bay, spills from the loom, fine enough that it could be liquid pouring across the floor.

Athena is thinking of all the women who weave. She thinks of Penelope weaving and unravelling, of Circe and Calypso weaving the functional or the decorative depending on what's needed. Each pragmatic in their own way.

The gods of Olympus have no need of pragmatism. Athena can weave for days, just to feel the fabric piling up around her feet and the endless threads winding around each other. There is no stopping to inspect the picture she has made, no unpicking a few regretted rows. There is only the back and forth. The ever-lengthening cloth.

Athena weaves as a meditation, to slip free of time. She told Arachne, another weaver, this once and Arachne laughed nastily. She thought that as a god Athena was already free of time, though the truth is that she is weighed down by the sheer volume of it.

If Athena had expected Arachne to be grateful
for to Athena for saving her life she had another
think coming. Arachne was not grateful to be
a spider, though her only other option was a
corpse. Still,

Athena found it hard to make friends and
Arachne was a captive audience, confined as she
was by her web.

The older I get, Athena had started to say to
Arachne, only to be interrupted with another
nasty laugh and another unpleasant truth that
as an immortal Athena didn't get older. There
was just more time piled up around her feet and
more of the endless threads winding around
each other.

You're one of my threads, Arachne, Athena
thinks, idly wondering where Arachne is.
Medusa is another thread. Athena knows where
she is. Statues tend not to wander off.

Athena is not proud of mistakes she made when
she was not young exactly, but less experienced.

That's it, she says aloud, she was right, I
am weighed down by the sheer volume of
experience. She speaks aloud to emphasise to
herself that no one is there. She is alone here,
outside of time.

Athena thinks of Arachne who no longer weaves but spins. She thinks of the miraculous geometry of Arachne's aerial lairs, jewelled in cold damp mornings. How much more beautiful Athena finds their incidental genius.

The older I get, she says aloud, the older I get.

Then there is only the sound of the loom and its various percussions. The shuttle, the beater and the treadle all moving in careful orchestration. Athena doesn't even need to think about the movements. She is so familiar with them that they perform themselves. She could do them in her sleep. She could do them backwards.

Not backwards, she thinks. Only forwards.

When there is so much time to live through only a fool would go back and redo a century, just in case there is an end waiting.

Just in case there is an end, she thinks. What if there isn't? She thinks of Penelope's shroud sitting folded on the shelf waiting for Laertes to die.

An end. A shape to give some definition. It is the hem that transforms fabric into a glorious robe. The tuck and the pin.

Athena stands up and walks away from the loom. The shuttle continues on its journey through the

warp, sure in its movements. And still the fabric
spills out, submerging the floor beneath waves
of silk.

Athena has a joke she saves for weddings, in case
she is called on to make a speech. The last time
she told it was at Peleus and Thetis' wedding, the
one Eris crashed. The one that started a war.
The war.

This is the joke.

Woman goes to the healer in Athens and says
she's depressed. Life seems cruel, pointless. She
is utterly bereft of purpose. Hope has deserted
her. The future terrifies her. The healer says,
Listen, Athena will be in the temple today, go
and see her, she'll know what to do, she knows
everything. And the woman says, But healer,
I am Athena.

The wedding guests always laugh because she is
the daughter of Zeus, dread conjuror of lightning
bolts and all that, and they are afraid of him.

She enjoys watching them laugh with their
gleeful mouths while their mirthless eyes dart
toward the All-father, trying to gauge when they
can stop laughing.

She enjoys knowing that one or two of them will
wake to think of her in the middle of the night,
in the black hours, and wonder if she really is
unhappy and if she is, how such a thing is even
possible. And if she is unhappy then surely they
too must be unhappy.

But most of all she enjoys the sound of the shuttle singing in the warp and the whisper of silk slipping over the flagstones.

there we were, we were sisters but
scattered on different islands
kept steady without our voices
shuttles chattering, quietening our wants

this was a community of sorts
but we deserve our place in society
our quickening signals must sing across oceans
gathering, gathering us together

THE ENSEMBLE

A WOMEN'S RALLY

Penelope waits. And she listens. She listens
because there is much wisdom in these words,
this back and forth, this cherished space, a secret
meeting place. Her voice, freed in this tiled room,
is strong and clear, joining the chorus of
sudden, unhindered laughter. Solidarity.
This public bathroom, clean and unassuming,
sings with chatter and oration equally,
a warm welcome for all ideas.
Whether the speaker must be high-minded or
the listener must be broad-minded, this is the
neat sanctuary, tucked away, seldom thought
of, only sought in times of distracting need.
But here and now, clean and safe: a concert hall,
a surgery, library and confessional.

It is that hope that brought Penelope here
to the fleet friendships found or forged in these
wasteful moments, these helpless minutes when
life is paused.

                        Penelope is surrounded,
no longer alone. These toilets are riotous
with Circe and Calypso comparing notes,
while Athena inspects her ageless face
and Scylla spills saltily over the top
of the end cubicle. *Just too much life for such
a tiny box*, neighbouring Melantho says
paddling suddenly in brine and seaweed.

And Penelope wonders where is the
fabled competition, the bitchy asides?
Where are the snide remarks and sidelong glances?
There is only an admired hand cream
shared, a safe taxi app recommended and
a word of comfort and encouragement.

And among these women, wherever
they might be found, Penelope is not wife,
mother, lover, bereft, left,
beloved, fidelity, she, woman, her,
woman. In this company she belongs to her
self. Still an undertaking, still unfinished
but no longer waiting for opening night,
listening for her cue, for when her line will fit.

In a moment it will be time for
one of them to leave, and another will arrive
to take her place among this chorus. But for
now Penelope leans against the cool, tiled wall
happy to wait her turn.

CONSTELLATIONS

Calypso listens. And she laughs. She laughs and
starts the whole room laughing again. Not that the
joke is particularly funny, it's more that
the recognition of such a truth is such
a joy. Although this joke *is* funny in its
own way, all the funnier for the wedding
guests' confusion. The comedian shrugs,
returns her gaze to the mirror and Calypso
rummages through her bag to find her hand
cream, turning out chargers and cables, pens
and scraps of paper, old envelopes tattooed
with scribbled lists, to do, to do, to do but
never done somehow. A hand appears, vaguely
scented, bearing the friendly offer to share.
It all seems eminently possible now,
a life of interests and curiosities,
of conversations and conferences. A life
of adventure.

          Calypso surveys the room,
all mortality and timeless time confused.
A world of differences, and yet so much
shared and to be shared. So many triumphs
and ideas, madcap plots and cunning plans.
So much to do that can be done, that's now possible,
so many strong hands dragging dark works into
the light, mending and setting and making good.

This work is impossible to do alone,
tucked away on islands, hidden from sight and
if it is true (and it is) that the only

way to win the fight is to get out of the
ring, then here is something to move towards,
to seek out. Company. A company of
souls. A victory.

         And now Calypso
is no longer just an island, not
even the only island in the room,
a whole world has opened up. Here is a
language shared, spoken widely even, loudly,
shouted from the rooftops to those who have an
ear, who have a mind to hear. Listen out now
for the call, be it to arms or prayer. Listen.

There is not long to wait now, Calypso thinks,
rubbing her hands together. Rosemary and
chamomile, a little cedar. *We have held
through all this wear, this tear and now there is not
much longer left to wait.*

ECDYSIS

Melantho breathes. And she counts. She counts the breaths,
one as she breathes in, two as she breathes out
and so on, up to a count of ten. And then
she starts again. One, two, three and then, even
though she is only half-listening, letting
the sounds come to her, she laughs at Athena's
joke. Well, not a joke more of a story and
not a funny story at that. More a
sort of veiled truth revealed in that way a
magician sweeps away a tablecloth leaving
crockery untouched. Like a held breath released.
Four, Melantho thinks as more of Scylla appears
under the partition between their cubicles
and the bracing sea breeze takes five, six, seven
and eight away in a burst of merry giggles.

This toilet had presented itself as an
escape at first. Empty, quiet but then full
and rowdy, but better for that. More alive,
more like life should be.

                         Melantho opens
the door and edges out into the crowded
area around the sinks and mirrors. Circe
makes a space for her, sliding up to Athena
who, elbow nudged, draws a neat black line from
the outer corner of her dark eye to her
temple with a stubby eyeliner. Athena
grins like lightning flashes and Melantho laughs.

This is a laugh that starts the room up again,
simple and uncomplicated, not a note
of cruelty in it.
Straightforward in its generosity.
The sound of watching a haughty sheep slip on a
banana skin and jump up unharmed. An
unexpected joy.

                    Not that joy should
be unexpected. Melantho now sets her
heart on a life bright with the expectation
of joy, bounding and tumbling in like a
puppy. In her pocket, her phone vibrates
and she is too busy laughing to answer it.

There is not much that cannot wait until the
end of a conversation or a story. Not
much that warrants careless interruption,
that will not wait for her.

BIOLUMINESCENCE

Scylla struggles. And she overcomes by seeping
under the partition, pooling around her
neighbour's feet. It is Melantho so there is
no issue, no shame or recrimination.
Scylla barks and hisses along when the others
laugh and no one remarks on how ill-mannered
or uncouth the sound. Scylla is not discordant
in this company. She is large, true and unkempt,
boisterously so, but welcome. Neither for
it or despite it, her size or sound, that is.
And if this cubicle is not big enough
that is not her fault, it is the fault of the
system that created this confining pen, of the
claustral minds that Scylla could snap in two with
one flick of her magnificent, bladed tongue.

Scylla regathers herself and draws herself
up to her full height, impeded completely
by the ceiling as if on an aeroplane
or in a jam jar.

                    She can see over the
cubicles all along the length of the sinks.
She rests her chins on the top of the
door and watches her friends. Yes, friends. They are all
together finally, no longer distanced
by sea or man and each the better for it.

Scylla's six sets of teeth gleam in the white light,
catching Circe's eye and Circe smiles back,
an easy smile, and then she gives a wink and

a wrinkling of her nose. This fondness is
a lens and through it Scylla can see herself
as she might hope to be seen: as a being
who is more.

More than a body but still a
body. Who is more than a mind but still a
mind. Who is self-defined but who is
embellished by others, elaborated.
An understanding shared, like an anecdote,
improved in the telling, each time funnier,
the twists more unexpected, the stakes higher.
More than a person yet still a person.

Scylla looks down at herself and although
she does not yet see what Circe seems to see,
she is learning to trust that wry, crinkly smile.
These changes take some time.

They wait. And they wait. And then they wait still more.
The inevitable queue navigates the
hallway like a brook, noisy and undeterred
by any obstacle or interruption.
Here is Alcmene, thumbs flashing across her phone
while Tyro offers unasked-for emoji advice.
Eriphyle fiddles with her necklace, watching
Ariadne and Phaedra perfecting some
dance move that neither she nor Epicaste
have heard of, or could do, or would need to do
but that nonetheless is fun to watch.

Maera, decided for now on her canine form,
waiting patiently in her capacity
as Anticleia's assistance dog, sniffs. Brine,
seaweed and shrimp.

Megara leans against the wall
and listens to the laughter from the toilets
and smiles. *What's funny?* Epicaste asks. Megara
explains. *If anyone makes me laugh I will pee
myself*, Epicaste says, *I'm not kidding*, and
Phaedra leaps as if to tickle her but doesn't and
this silliness does not diminish this most
promising of all things: a group of women, idle.

Tyro, near the front, swaps places with Epicaste.
She can see that Penelope has reached
her destination. The whole queue shifts forward.
Alcmene and Ariadne exchange the weighty
responsibility of holding the door

open as easily as shaking hands with
an old family friend.

                    Anticleia, though
older than the rest, less spry and spritely than
she might like, has got the same kind of giggles
that attack small children and generously
she passes them on until the whole line is
fidgety with an unspecific mirth. But
Anticleia is older than the rest and
knows that there is fire here, banked down but burning.

Maera lies down to pass the wait in sleep.
Eyes closed, hairy chin tucked between neat paws she
dreams briefly of stars, of Procyon, and of
sheer cliffs. Risks and rewards.

FEVERFEW

Circe examines. She examines her face
in the mirror and wonders when the precise
moment came that it no longer matched what was
inside. Now, given the space to breathe, to look
around and take stock, she is counting up the
experiences and cannot see each one
etched into her face like the marks on a cell wall
counting time served. Age has not touched her but
life has definitely kept score. Calypso
will never find a anything in that bag so
Circe passes her some homemade hand cream.
There is beautiful Scylla and here comes Melantho.
And there goes Athena's eyeliner. Circe
is newly headlong, living at some pace, a
firework fizzing off towards the woodshed.

She had always felt that time alone would be
not a solution, but a salve and yet here
she is with no space for elbows but – finally! –
room to breathe.

                    Penelope slips into
a cubicle and new faces appear around
the door. *There are so many of us.* Circe
does not mean to speak out loud but Athena,
her own face repaired, smiles and says something about
an old army that Circe does not hear
because Phaedra and Ariadne are singing
a song about independence and handbags.

And there is suddenly so much life crammed
into this tiny, unloved room. It reminds
Circe of a time, far away now, when she was
taken to a library and, standing at the
start of the bookshelves, stretching ahead of her
like a maze, she felt overwhelmed by all the
possible futures within reach.

                              And now what?
Circe adjusts her cuffs, buttons her cardigan
and begins to get her things together. She picks
up the small blue raffle ticket and slips it
into her pocket, feeling lucky. Calypso is talking
about getting a drink after the celebrations
finish, she knows a great place. Quiet, tucked away,
just to unwind after the excitement. Reflect.

And Circe hears the chorus of enthusiastic voices
wondering at her own as it joins in, saying
Yeah, that sounds great! I'd really love to come along!
Because this most frightening thing, a group of women,
is no monster after all.

POLIAS

Athena breathes. And she counts. She counts the breaths
and then forgets what number she is on
because she has allowed herself to feel the
very specific happiness of having
made a room laugh. Not because a joke is
particularly funny, or even a joke
really, but the joy of recognition, a
shared experience. How unexpected, she
thinks, really, noticing all the differences
between them first, the skin, the hair, the heights,
the money, the lives. Even the loftiest
of us shit. Now she is thinking about gold-plated
bidets and how she should focus on how near
this pencil is to her eye before something goes wrong.
Circe nudges her as if just thinking it made it so.

It is not easy to relax in this space,
it is not so protected as to make a body
like Athena feel safe but still, her place is
claimed, owned.

                    Circe is very apologetic,
when there isn't any need. The slashing black
line is easily dealt with and Athena moves
on to fixing her errant hair. Scylla is
watching them over her tiny stall and Athena
is arrested by the sublime force of the
woman, caught as if in a sudden downpour,
torrential and dramatic, all-consuming.

Athena tries to imagine a world in which
it is not Penelope that is beautiful,
but abundant Scylla. How many
of these tiny rebellions would fire
a revolution?

Penelope appears
at the edge of Athena's vision like an
admonishment and Athena hears Phaedra's
surprising alto and Ariadne's bright
treble and wants to hear a whole choir of voices.
Responsibility is draw to Athena
like static to silk. She makes decisions like mortals
offer prayers – less nowadays but on insistent
occasions the clamour can be deafening.

What should she do now? Then Calypso takes the lead,
with her offer of pale ales and elaborate gins.
And Penelope shouts over the toilet door
that she's in, then they're all in. No one left behind,
shut up or out.

And effort falls away to ease.

sleep now, my brave ones, sleep
& in the crisply laundered morning
we can re-tell ourselves again

DAWN

Dawn will soon be here. Her strong hands are gathering skeins of light.
It will not be long before she breaches the curve of the horizon, her threads
will weave the next day from this old night, figuring patterns this way
& that, until the fretful small hours are unravelled & made
into another beginning. The old shrouded in the new. What story
will this new day tell? Whose voices will emerge from this ornate quiet?

39.6243° N, 19.9217° E

Now, already minutes older, Dawn stalks through pools of darkness & disquiet
like a cat about to pounce on some loose twitching yarn, her footsteps light
on the soundless air until she can wait no longer to burst upon the story.
Twilight is under her sharp claws, quicksilver tangled, all pulled threads
& the early morning stains the low sky, fulfilment of a promise made.
We inch forward, brightness pressing at the dull grey edge to mark the way.

I confess I want more from this Dawn. I want a searing light to burn away these footprints & their past paths. I want to start again in peace & quiet. I want a new, clean world, not a newly cleaned one, like an old blanket made of patches. This is the small hours thinking, a narrow pool of lamplight casting only the light to see seconds ahead. Holes are all dropped threads can leave, space for us to slip through, to fall away into ancient history.

Dawn does not take requests, of course, she continues to tell her daily story,
arrowing her gleam across the star-stippled sky in the same way
as she always has done. She clothes the sky but does not tailor the threads
that she has woven. I will stitch a button to keep me from the cold quiet.
Wait & see, Dawn says, but she has the faith of the masterful, featherlight
& easy, her passage is familiar, she follows a path she's already made.

Perhaps this is the best of the world, this dawn, this day remade.
Like a page rubbed clean but still bearing some trace of the other story,
night's shadows scattered to make space for new ones drawn by sunlight.
All the possibility of a reclaimed ball of yarn & an empty loom, which way
the pattern will fall still to be discovered. But for now, everything is quiet,
poised on the blade of the present, the past & the future unspliced threads.

50.8191° N, 0.1520° W

I promise that whatever I make will be returned to unravelled threads,
the ends hanging free or else tucked into the neatly wound hank, made
tidy for next time, for new hands to pick up & weave new cloth. Quiet
patterns or vivid, whichever works. Penelope is waiting for her story
to be retold, holding off time by unpicking each day's work to keep a way
out alive & now she's beginning to weave again in the opaline light.

Listen in the early morning hush. Only my busy shuttle & its threads
sing in the vanishing twilight, industriously remaking what had been made
& will be remade again.

A story is always unfinished anyway

GLOSSARY OF

TITLES AND WOMEN

adze: a tool used for cutting and shaping large pieces of wood. It looks similar to an axe but has an arched blade at right angles to its handle.

agapē: (ancient Greek) unconditional love.

Alcmene: the granddaughter of Perseus and Andromeda and mother of Heracles. Heracles' father is Zeus, who disguised himself as Alcmene's husband.

alder: a tree. Alder wood does not rot in water and was historically used in shipbuilding.

anthurium: an exotic houseplant with poisonous sap that causes irritation to the skin and eyes.

Anticleia: Odysseus' mother, the literal translation of her name is 'without fame'.

Arachne: challenged Athena to a weaving competition and was turned into a spider.

archaia: (ancient Greek) ancient.

Argos: a city in the Peloponnese, Greece. Argos is also the name of Odysseus' dog.

Ariadne: a princess who helped to kill her half-brother, the Minotaur, and eloped with Theseus who then abandoned her on Naxos. Phaedra's sister.

Athena: the Greek goddess of wisdom and war. Daughter of Zeus. She was not born in the conventional way; she leaped fully formed from her father's head.

bioluminescence: the production and emission of light by living organisms, particularly common in marine creatures and fungi.

brocade: a richly decorated shuttle-woven fabric, often using gold or silver threads.

Calypso: a nymph, witch and weaver living on Ogygia. Odysseus stayed with her for seven years until Zeus and Athena plotted his return to Ithaca, thus saving him from his terrible homesickness. Often confused with Circe.

cape lilac: a poisonous plant causing loss of appetite, vomiting, constipation or diarrhoea, bloody faeces, stomach pain, pulmonary congestion, cardiac arrest, rigidity, lack of coordination and general weakness. Death usually occurs after twenty-four hours.

cardinal: a small red bird whose appearance in dreams is thought to bring a message from a loved one who has died.

castor bean: a plant with extremely poisonous seeds that are a source of ricin. Symptoms include a burning sensation in the mouth and throat, abdominal pain, purging and bloody diarrhoea. Severe dehydration will result in death within several days.

caulk: a material used to stop seams and joints from leaking.

Circe: a minor goddess, witch and weaver living on Aeaea. Odysseus landed on her island uninvited and she used her talent in potions and spells to turn his invading sailors into pigs.

columbine: a plant with highly poisonous seeds and roots that contain cardiogenic toxins which cause severe gastroenteritis and heart palpitations that are often fatal.

crake: any marsh birds of the family Rallidae, though the term usually refers to the small, short-billed rails.

cryptadia: (ancient Greek) things to be kept hidden.

Dawn: the personification of dawn in *The Odyssey*; the Greek goddess of morning is Eos.

deadly nightshade: a plant with berries that cause delirium and hallucinations.

ecdysis: (ancient Greek) the act of shedding a hard outer layer, like an insect does.

eider: a large sea duck. The ancient Greek root of its name means wool.

epaulia: (ancient Greek) the day after the marriage ceremony when the gifts are presented.

Epicaste: mother, and wife, of Oedipus.

Eriphyle: persuaded her husband to become one of the Seven of Thebes in exchange for the Necklace of Harmonia, knowing that he would die. She was murdered by their son.

fastness: a material's resistance to fading or running.

feverfew: a plant used as a treatment for headaches and migraines.

figure: the pattern, design or decoration of a fabric.

gimlet: a hand tool for drilling holes.

hygiene: (ancient Greek) cleanliness.

jaeger: a dark coloured gull also known as a skua.

klēros: (ancient Greek) an inheritance, especially one bestowed through a systemic law such as a dowry.

Kriophoros: the ram-bearer, sometimes the 'Good Shepherd'.

kylix: (ancient Greek) a shallow drinking cup with two handles.

larkspur: a meadow plant causing severe digestive discomfort and skin irritation.

lymnaea: a genus of air-breathing freshwater snail.

Maera: there are several Maeras in ancient Greek mythology. Among them was a hound belonging to Icarius's daughter, Erigone. Another was a daughter of Atlas and another, a daughter of the river god Erasinus. .

mandrake: a plant which causes blurred vision, dilation of the pupils, dryness of the mouth, difficulty in urinating, dizziness, headaches, vomiting, blushing, a rapid heart rate, hyperactivity and hallucinations.

marsh marigold: a plant which may cause convulsions, burning of the throat, vomiting, bloody diarrhoea, dizziness, fainting, blistering and inflammation of the skin, and gastric illness.

meadow saffron: a flowering plant also known as the 'autumn crocus' or 'naked ladies', the effects of its poison are similar to arsenic and there is no known antidote.

Melantho: a slave in Penelope's household.

Mentes: King of the Taphians. Athena disguises herself as Mentes in *The Odyssey* while guiding Telemachus.

Mentor: a friend of Odysseus who provides guidance to Telemachus while his father is away. Athena disguises herself as him in *The Odyssey* while visiting Ithaca.

moirai: (ancient Greek) an individual's destiny as decided by the will of the gods.

mountain arnica: a plant causing stomach pain, diarrhoea, vomiting and contact dermatitis.

night-heron: a type of heron. The genus name Nycticorax derives from the Ancient Greek for "night raven".

obol: a coin placed on the eyes of the dead to pay for their passage across the river Styx and into the underworld.

oikos: (ancient Greek) home.

oleander: a plant causing nausea and vomiting, excess salivation, abdominal pain, bloody diarrhoea, irregular heart rate (a racing heart which then slows to below normal), poor or irregular circulation, drowsiness, tremors or shaking of the muscles, seizures, collapse and fatal coma.

oriole: a family of small, often brightly coloured birds that symbolise friendship.

pagliacci: clown.

Pallas: daughter of the sea-god Triton and a childhood friend of Athena. Athena accidentally killed her during a friendly sparring match and took the epithet Pallas in her grief.

pankration: (ancient Greek) a form of wrestling where anything is permitted except biting, gouging or attacking the genitals.

Penelope: Odysseus' wife and another weaver.

peplos: a sleeveless outer garment worn by women in Ancient Greece.

Phaedra: now one of the most famous women in Greek mythology, but most relevantly: she is the wife of Theseus and sister of Ariadne.

Polias: an epithet given to Athena, referring to her role as guardian of the city of Athens.

quelea: a small bird in the weaver family. The red-billed quelea is thought to be the most numerous species of bird in the world.

rail: a marsh bird and type of crake.

rosary pea: a poisonous plant causing nausea, vomiting, convulsions, liver failure and, after several days, death. It is twice as powerful as ricin.

Scylla: once a sea nymph, now a sea monster. In some versions of her story Circe poisoned the pool that transformed her.

sett: the number of threads in the warp and weft of a fabric, measured per inch.

storm-petrel: a sea bird thought to be a bad omen; some believed they were the souls of dead sailors.

thimbleweed: a poisonous plant causing blistering and inflammation of the mouth, indigestion, diarrhoea and vomiting.

tram: a thread made by twisting two or three silk yarns together.

trechein: (ancient Greek) to run or move quickly.

twist: the amount of twist in a yarn affects how the fabric feels and how fast it is.

Tyro: her narrative almost epitomises that of women in mythology. She is raped by a god (not Zeus this time, but Poseidon), murders some of her children and gets no credit for setting in motion the chain of events that start a major narrative arc, the Golden Fleece. She marries two of her uncles, one of whom is Sisyphus.

warp: the threads of a fabric that run the length of the fabric on the loom and are woven with weft.

water hemlock: an extremely toxic plant causing seizures that result in a decrease in the pH of the blood, swelling in the brain, blood coagulation disorders, muscle breakdown and kidney failure. Symptoms also include ECG abnormalities, wheezing and respiratory distress, hallucinations, delirium, coma and drooling.

weft: the threads of a fabric that run across the width of the fabric on the loom and are woven with warp.

white snakeroot: the toxins in this plant are passed to humans through cow's milk. Symptoms include trembling, vomiting and severe intestinal pain.

wolfsbane: when eaten this plant will initially cause vomiting and diarrhoea. This will be followed by burning, tingling and numbness, and then motor weakness. Also, hypotension and arrhythmia, sweating, dizziness, difficulty breathing, headache and confusion. Death usually occurs with two to six hours and a post-mortem examination will determine the cause of death as asphyxia.

xenia: (ancient Greek) the concept of hospitality.

yarn: often referred to as thread, the basic component of any fabric.

Valentine Carter grew up in a small village, escaped to the city and now lives by the sea. They recently completed an MA in creative writing at Birkbeck, University of London, where they are now studying for a PHD. Valentine has short fiction published by *The Fiction Pool*, *Bandit Fiction*, *In Yer Ear* and *The Mechanics' Institute Review:* Issue 15 and Issue 16, and poetry published by *Perverse* and *Visual Verse*. This is their debut novel.